the shadows trilogy, book one

SHADOWS OF JANE

amy hale

To Jennifer,
Enjoy exploring the shadows!.
xoxo,
Amy Hale

Shadows of Jane
The Shadows Trilogy, Book One
Amy Hale
Copyright © 2015 Amy Hale
All rights reserved.

Cover Designer: Sarah Hansen, Okay Creations,
www.okaycreations.com
Editor and Interior Designer: Jovana Shirley, Unforeseen Editing,
www.unforeseenediting.com

ISBN-13: 978-1511529778

OTHER BOOKS BY AMY HALE

Ulterior Motives

Catching Whitney

For strong women everywhere
and my late mother, Janice McGuire, the strongest woman I've ever known.
I love and miss you, Mom!

CONTENTS

ONE

I RUN FROM SHADOWS.

THEY CALL MY NAME AND TAUNT ME WITH THEIR CRIES.

She ran. She ran as fast and as far as her legs would carry her. Stumbling through the trees, she squinted and wiped the rain from her eyes. Exhaustion had begun to overtake her limbs, and she was unsure of how much farther she could go. She stopped, doubled over, and grasped her trembling knees for support. Her breath came in short, shallow gasps as she attempted to recover from the exertion. Her lungs burned, and it felt like they would explode if she didn't slow down. Despite her need for rest, her mind screamed at her to keep going. She needed to get away. She had to put as much distance as possible between herself and them.

The faint sounds of running footsteps from somewhere behind her spurred her into action once again. As she dashed through the dense forest, she frantically searched for somewhere to hide. There was no way she could continue to outrun them. Eventually, she would get caught. Her only hope was to hide away and pray they passed by her. The idea of spending the night in the forest was terrifying, but she was even more frightened at the thought of them taking her back. She would never go back—ever.

Her pace slowed as she noticed a large brush pile. She quietly worked her way past several fallen branches and peered into the mound of limbs and twigs. Hidden behind it was the mouth of what appeared to be a small cave. It didn't look to be very spacious, but she hoped it would be enough so that she could disappear from sight until the hunting party moved on. With any luck, they'd never notice the modest cavern. Unfortunately, luck hadn't been on her side for years.

She pulled just enough of the pile out of the way, so her slight frame could scamper into the darkness. Then, she reached forward and did her best to pull the limbs back into place. Scooting farther into the cold, bleak cavity, she settled herself in between an icy dirt wall and a large rock. With her legs drawn to her chest, she pressed her cheek to her knees and closed her eyes. She was soaked to the bone and would probably end up with hypothermia. But if she were going to die, it would at least be her way and not by the sadistic hands of those searching for her.

She closed her eyes and tried to envision her childhood home and the parents she missed so badly. It had been years since she saw them—almost ten to be exact. She wondered if she could find them after all this time.

Are they still alive?

Her thoughts unintentionally wandered to the night she had been taken from the only two people who truly loved her for who she was. To them, she was special and someone to be treasured.

To those in the search party, she was an oddity. She was their plaything. Today's escape had changed all that. She refused to let them control her ever again. She'd rather die first.

She sat in silence and waited. For several minutes, nothing could be heard, except for the wind and the light patter of rain striking the dead leaves littering the forest floor. Her pulse beat erratically as she waited for any indication that they'd found her hiding place.

Her heart almost stopped when she finally heard them.

"Where the hell did she go?" a gruff voice shouted.

"I don't know. She couldn't have gotten too far," replied a less masculine voice.

"Stupid little twit! I'll make her pay for this!" said a woman, her voice filled with venom.

"Come on. She probably headed toward the creek," the gruff voice said.

She sat there, frozen, daring not to breathe, as she heard them walking away.

Even after an hour or so, she was still afraid to move. She was unsure if they were really gone or if they were trying to trick her into feeling secure so that she'd exit her hiding spot.

She hoped that, maybe just this once, fortune was shining down on her.

It had grown completely dark, so she wrapped her arms around herself for warmth and curled into the fetal position on the dirt floor. If she survived the night, she could plan her next step. For now, she needed sleep.

She awoke the next morning to bright sunshine filtering through the brush and the sound of chirping birds. Her legs were stiff and cold, so she stretched and cautiously crawled out from behind the rock. Once near the cave entrance, she poked her head out and took in her surroundings. Seeing no signs of human life, she slowly wriggled out between the branches and then guardedly made her way through the trees, heading north, until she stopped at a steep ridge. She smiled at the sight before her, hope filling her heart for the first time in years.

Just a little longer, and I should be safe.

She'd taken only three steps down the sharp incline when she suddenly lost her footing and tumbled headfirst all the way to the bottom of the hillside.

Colt Henderson looked down at his muddy boots and sighed. He was really tired of fixing his dad's beat-up old truck. The 1974 Ford F-100 was practically falling apart, but his dad never considered trading it in for a newer model, no matter how much Colt had tried to convince him. He smiled as he remembered his dad's argument for not buying a replacement.

"They don't make them like this anymore, son. Why would I want one of those newfangled contraptions with computers and such? It'd cost more to fix and have more to break down! Just a waste of good money when we can easily make the small repairs on this one instead."

What Colt hadn't understood at the time was that his father could barely afford to fix the old vehicle, let alone buy a new one.

Randy Henderson had been a proud man, and while he had known it was obvious they were a poor family, he would never have admitted it out loud. Instead, he had given reasonable excuses as to why they couldn't do this or buy that. His boys, Colt and Brett, never had the heart to argue with their old man, so they would just let it be.

Colt glanced at the mostly rusty blue pickup. He didn't think it was going to hold out much longer. Even if he could keep the engine running, the body was disintegrating. Regardless of finances, his dad had loved that old truck, so Colt would keep it running for as long as possible, if only to help him feel closer to the man he'd recently lost. Randy hadn't always been the easiest man to live with, but he was the only parent Colt and his brother had known for most of their childhoods.

Colt shut the hood and walked around to the tailgate, cleaning his hands with a rag. He repacked the toolbox and slid it behind the bench seat in the cab.

Once everything was back in place, he gave the old pickup a frustrated pat on the side. "Hang with me a bit longer, baby. I'm not ready to retire you just yet."

Colt glanced toward the pile of firewood he'd chopped earlier, which was still sitting on the small porch of his father's modest hunting shack. Winter was mostly over, yet today there was a chill in the air, and he really needed to get a fire going.

That little building had been Randy's pride and joy. He'd built the small cabin from the ground up and loved bringing his boys out here for hunting and fishing. Colt had to admit that some of his best memories were from weekends spent in the hills of Kentucky with his father teaching them how to live off the land. It was part of why Colt was here now.

Colt thought back to his dad's funeral. It had been a small and simple gathering. Randy had specifically told the boys he didn't want anything fancy or expensive, so they had given him a nice, intimate send-off. Then, Brett had gone back to college, and Colt had gone back to work as a mechanic at Mike's Bikes.

Motorcycles were Colt's life, and while it wasn't a six-figure kind of job, he loved what he did. His boss, Mike, was a dick, but after six years there, Colt knew how to handle him.

Surprisingly, even Mike had realized that Colt wasn't properly dealing with the loss of his dad, and he never noticed anything that wouldn't personally benefit him. Colt had threatened to take Jerry, his coworker, out at the knees for touching his tools. After that incident, Mike had suggested Colt take a few days off.

Thinking back, Colt realized that it might have been more for Jerry's safety than his own well-being. Either way, Colt really didn't give a crap. He had an extra week off—with pay—and he was going to enjoy it.

As he walked toward the cabin, Colt shook his head and smirked. He was pretty sure that weasel Jerry had pissed his pants when Colt confronted him. That was a memory Colt felt sure would keep a smile on his face for weeks to come. Colt wasn't a mean guy. He just had no patience for jackasses. And Jerry was a colossal jackass. Colt suspected that Jerry slapped his girlfriend around, and if Colt ever personally witnessed such actions, he'd ensure that Jerry never hit anyone ever again.

Once near the door, Colt loaded his arms with firewood and went inside. He placed some crumpled newspapers and a few of the logs on the grate, and then he lit the papers.

When heat was finally radiating from the fireplace, he made a cup of coffee and sat down to go through a trunk of family items his dad had left behind. Colt had just pulled out a small shoebox when he thought he heard a knock.

He froze. *A knock? How could there be a knock? There are no other cabins for miles.*

He heard it again. He rose and quietly approached the door, grabbing his dad's twelve-gauge shotgun along the way.

For the third time, Colt heard a faint knock on the cabin door. He yanked open the door to find a wet and somewhat malnourished petite young lady leaning against his doorframe. Her red hair was dirty and matted to her face, and her clothes were torn and ragged.

She looked up with piercing green eyes that quickly registered surprise upon seeing him. "Who are you?" she asked softly.

"Excuse me?" Colt replied. "Can I help you?"

She nodded once and then leaned in close. "Where are they?" she whispered.

He was completely confused. "They? Who are you talking about?"

She put her hand on her forehead in a gesture of despair and then closed her eyes. "I-I don't know." She ran her hand through her hair and winced when she hit a sore spot.

Colt placed the gun just inside the door and then crossed his arms as he looked at the presumably high young lady before him. "Are you lost? Where did you come from?" He tried not to sound harsh, but he had no tolerance for addicts.

She gazed up at him once more, a tear making a clean trail down one dirt-stained cheek. She pulled her hand away from her head and stared at her palm.

Concerned about the sudden lack of color in her face, Colt glanced at her hand and noticed the presence of blood on her fingers. She took a step back and then wavered, unsteady on her feet. Colt rushed forward and caught her just as she collapsed.

Two

Colt looked down at the unconscious girl in his arms. She didn't look a day over sixteen, but then she also looked like she hadn't taken very good care of herself. She was thin, and as he lifted her, he realized she was even lighter than she looked. His mind raced about her possible circumstances as he carefully placed her limp body on a small sofa near the fireplace.

Squatting down next to her, he felt her forehead. He thought she felt warm, despite the fact that she seemed to be shivering now, but he wasn't exactly a nurse, and he couldn't recall seeing a thermometer in the cabin at any time. It wasn't one of those things his dad had considered a necessity when they spent time here. Colt grabbed a blanket off a nearby chair and draped it over her.

What am I doing? I don't know what's wrong with her, and even if I did, I wouldn't know how to help. She needs a doctor.

Letting out an audible sigh, he searched his jacket for his cell phone. Hitting the name *Dr. Weston* in his Contacts, he stared at the girl and muttered to himself, "So much for my week of rest and relaxation."

"Hello? Dr. Weston speaking."

"Doc, it's Colt Henderson. I have a situation."

"A situation? Like what?"

"Uh…well, there's a girl passed out on my sofa."

"That's hardly a situation you can't handle, Colt. Don't you often have women staying over?" Dr. Weston gave a small laugh.

"No, Doc, not that kind of passed out. I mean, unconscious. I'm at the cabin. She knocked on the door, mumbled something weird, and then collapsed. I don't know what to do."

"Oh, dear. You need to get her to the hospital as soon as possible."

"Swell. I'll be there as quickly as I can. Should take me about thirty minutes."

"See you then."

Colt hung up and stuffed the phone back into the pocket of his jacket, and then he slipped it on. He ran out to start the truck, and he laid an extra blanket and a pillow on the bench seat. Leaving the door open, he ran back inside to get her. Wrapping her in the blanket he'd previously draped over her, he carefully carried her to the truck and placed her inside. She let out a slight moan, but she didn't otherwise appear to have regained consciousness.

After grabbing a couple of bottles of water and some beef jerky, in case she woke up dehydrated or hungry, he locked up the cabin and got in the driver's seat. He had to carefully move her head as he climbed in, and then he tried to situate her until she wasn't quite so cramped. She surprised him by grabbing the blanket and curling into a fetal position, her eyes still closed.

He drove away from the cabin as fast as he could safely travel while he worried that getting her to the hospital could mean life or death for her. Colt also feared he'd already wasted precious time by calling the doctor. He didn't know this girl from Adam, but he would feel bad if something happened to her because he'd reacted too slowly.

He'd been driving for about fifteen minutes when she moaned again and started to sit up a little. He wasn't sure what to expect from her, so he tried to keep an eye on her and on the road. She pushed herself upright, and then she leaned back and pulled the blanket up toward her neck. Colt couldn't believe that through all of this, she never once appeared to open her eyes. She just sat up and got as comfortable as possible, and then she seemed to go right back to sleep—or whatever she was doing. Once she settled and didn't move again for several moments, he relaxed and focused on the drive once more.

He still had another ten minutes or so before he'd reach town. The good news was, she seemed to be in less danger than he'd originally suspected, so maybe she'd be okay in the long run. He was lost in thought when he felt her snuggle up to him as she laid her head on his shoulder. Her feet were tucked up under her legs with only her toes sticking out of bloody, torn socks.

Colt loudly cleared his throat, hoping she'd wake up and realize how awkward their positions were. He'd never willfully push a pretty girl away from him, but this wasn't the bar scene. For all he knew, she wasn't even old enough to enter a bar.

When did I start thinking she was pretty?

He blew out a frustrated breath. This girl was ill and injured, and the last thing she needed was him thinking lewd thoughts about her—not that he was, but he knew how easily his mind could wander in that direction.

8

No one could ever accuse Colt Henderson of being a saint. He wasn't evil, but he sure as hell wasn't going to win any awards for community service or good deeds. This situation was the closest he'd come to being a Good Samaritan in years.

He pulled the truck up to the double doors at the ER and honked the horn. Two men in uniform came out, and Colt pointed to the girl curled up beside him.

Lance, one of Colt's classmates from high school, came around to the driver's window. "What'd ya do now, Colt?"

"Don't give me crap right now, Lance. Get a damn gurney or wheelchair, and get this girl inside."

Lance nodded and motioned above the truck to the other man. "Wheelchair, Greg!"

Greg ran back inside while Colt gave Lance the same details he'd given to Dr. Weston. Lance trotted around to the other side of the truck and opened the door.

Then, he tried to audibly rouse the young woman curled up next to Colt. "Hey, sweetheart. Can you wake up for us? We need to get you out of the truck."

Colt watched, but she didn't respond. When Greg still hadn't pushed the wheelchair through the automatic doors, he became impatient. "Oh, for—just let me do it!"

He opened his door and turned toward her. Then, he scooted himself off the seat, and he managed to get his arms under her body. He picked her up and carried her through the doors. Lance was a few feet behind him, saying something about not leaving his truck in the loading zone. Colt couldn't care less. This girl needed help, and the truck could wait.

Monica, the receptionist behind the desk, gave Colt a big smile, which faded once she saw the girl in his arms. Her eyebrows rose above her wide blue eyes. "Who's that?"

"I have no idea, but she needs medical attention."

Monica picked up a clipboard and walked around to the front of the counter. "Follow me."

They passed several small exam rooms until they reached one in the back where she motioned for Colt to enter. He placed the girl in the bed and covered her back up, taking a somewhat protective stance by her side. He didn't know why he felt the need to stick around. He'd done his duty. But something kept him glued in place.

Maybe she'll need to see a familiar face when she wakes up.

Who am I kidding? She saw me for, like, thirty seconds. I won't be familiar to her at all.

Within a few minutes, a nurse took her temperature, confirming she did indeed have a fever, and proclaimed that her pulse was a little weak.

Colt was anxious for the doctor. "Where the hell is Doc? He said he'd be waiting!"

The nurse gave him a smile. "Don't worry. He'll be here as soon as he can." She stepped forward and placed a reassuring hand on his arm. "Why don't you have a seat until he gets here? I'm sure your girlfriend will be just fine."

Colt shook his head, feeling too antsy to sit. "She's not my girlfriend. I don't even know her."

The nurse gave him an odd look but nodded. "Suit yourself. He'll be right in."

Just as the nurse was leaving, Lance entered. "There you are. You gotta move your truck, man. It's gonna get towed if you don't."

Colt shot an annoyed look at Lance. "You move it. I'm not leaving this room."

Lance glared at Colt. "You're such a jackass sometimes." Then, he left, complaining loudly about how he wasn't a valet.

Colt paced near her bedside until Dr. Weston entered the room. He was a middle-aged man with a portly physique and a receding hairline. Colt always thought if Dr. Weston gained another fifty pounds, he'd look like Boss Hogg from those old *Dukes of Hazzard* shows. Thankfully, the man was a medical genius, and Colt knew if anyone could help this mystery girl, Dr. Weston could.

She still hadn't moved or made a sound since Colt brought her in.

Placing a stethoscope on her heart, Dr. Weston began his examination. Once he was finished looking her over, he called in the nurse to start an IV.

"Her temperature is high, and she has a nasty gash on her head. I'm pretty sure she hasn't had a proper meal in months. I'm going to admit her and hope we can figure out her story. Once she wakes up, maybe she'll tell us what we need to know."

Colt just nodded, staring at the frail figure on the bed. He stepped out of the way while a nurse inserted the IV and prepared her for her trip upstairs to a private room. Even as he fell back and watched from a distance, he felt a possessive pull to stay close by. Aside from his kid brother, he couldn't recall ever feeling this protective.

Maybe that's it. She's like the little sister I never had.

Dr. Weston interrupted Colt's thoughts, "We'll do blood work, run some tests, and make sure it's nothing a round of antibiotics can't cure. Then, we'll keep her fed and healthy until we can notify her family."

"Thanks, Doc."

Colt reluctantly left the room and made it halfway down the hall when Monica caught up to him.

"Colt! We need you to fill out these forms for her."

"I can't, Monica. I don't know anything about her."

10

Monica glanced at the papers in her hand. "Hmm…I guess she'll be Jane Doe for now. I'll have her fill them out once she's awake. Would you like me to call you when she wakes up?"

Colt's mind raced. He should walk away now while he can, while he's not too involved. He should run back to his cabin and enjoy the rest of his vacation time. He should—

"Yes," he said, surprising himself. "Please let me know what you can."

Monica nodded at him and walked to her desk just in time to answer the phone.

Colt left through the double doors he'd entered in and searched for his truck. He quickly spotted it all the way at the far end of the lot. To no one in particular, he said, "Thanks for moving my truck, Lance. You're a douche."

Jane Doe woke up to lights shining in her face.

Ouch! Too bright!

She used the back of her hand to shield her eyes from the invading light. Once she seemed to adjust, she took stock of her surroundings.

A hospital? Why am I in a hospital?

She couldn't seem to remember how she'd gotten there or why she was there. In fact, she couldn't remember anything at all. She closed her eyes and tried to will the memories to appear, but nothing happened. Panicked, she started visually searching the room for anything that would give her a clue about herself and her situation.

The beeping of the heart monitor next to her bed was quickly getting on her nerves. In a fit of anger and anxiety, she unplugged it. Immediately, she enjoyed the satisfaction of the quietness until a nurse came rushing in to see why she'd flatlined. Giving her a stern look, she found the plug and set the machine back up.

"Nice to see you are finally awake. How are you feeling?"

Jane shrugged and peered at the nurse's name tag that said *Camille.* "Okay, I guess. How long have I been out?"

Camille picked up the chart from the foot of the bed and wrote down some notes. "Only a few days." Then, she placed the chart on the bedside table and took a few steps toward Jane. "I need to check your temperature. Open up, please."

Jane allowed Camille to take her temperature, and to the nurse's delight, it was normal.

"Very good," she said. She picked the chart back up and scribbled more notes.

As Camille started to walk away, Jane grabbed her arm. "Please tell me, how did I get here? Who am I?" Tears were quickly pooling in her vivid green eyes as she begged the nurse for anything that would set her world right.

Camille's eyes grew wide. "Oh, dear." She patted Jane's hand. "I'll go get the doctor, and we'll both be right back. Don't worry, sweetheart." Then, she quickly breezed out of the room with the faint mutterings of, "Dear Lord. Poor girl," lingering behind her.

Jane leaned her head back against the pillows and closed her eyes, hoping that this nightmare would be over when she opened them.

Within minutes, Camille returned with Dr. Weston.

He gave her a friendly smile as he looked at her chart, and then he pulled a nearby chair close to the bed. "Hello, young lady. I'm Dr. Weston. I'm very glad to see you doing so well. You gave us a good scare the first day you were in here."

"I did?"

"Yes indeed. You were severely dehydrated. You were running a high fever, and you had a gash on your head, cuts and scrapes on your hands, feet, and knees, but that wasn't the worst of it. You actually died on us at one point. It was…well, never mind that. Look at you now! You're awake with color in your cheeks, and from the looks of it, you're doing very well."

"Thanks, I guess." Jane had no idea how to reply. Her confusion was short-circuiting her ability to be logical.

Dr. Weston leaned forward, bracing his forearms against his legs. "Nurse Camille tells me you have questions. I can't promise to have all the answers, but I'll be glad to tell you what I can."

Jane swallowed a lump in her throat. "I don't remember anything. I don't know how I got here or how I got hurt. I don't even remember my own name."

Giving her a sad smile, he nodded slowly. "Unfortunately, I can't answer most of those things for you. What I do know is that you must have taken a nasty fall, your temperature was dangerously high, and your heart stopped for several minutes. Combined, it could be why you have lost your memories. Your brain might not be ready to deal with the recent trauma."

All she could manage to say was, "Oh, okay." Then, she studied her fingers, as if they could somehow tell her all the secrets locked away in her mind.

Dr. Weston stood and handed the chart to Camille. "Don't worry yourself over it too much. Your memories could reappear at any time. The brain is a funny thing, and it surprises us every day. Between you and me, I think there is something a little unique about you. I can't put my finger on it, but I've witnessed miracles before." He looked directly into her eyes. "I'm looking at a miracle right now."

She smiled at him, her first smile since waking up in this horrific ordeal. "Thank you, doctor. What do I…" She hesitated.

"It's okay. Ask any questions you have."

"I don't know my name. What should I have people call me until I get my memories back?"

Dr. Weston scratched his chin. "I suppose you can use anything you like."

"What have you all been calling me?"

He smiled at her again. "Well, we've named you Jane Doe since we didn't have any other information."

She thought for a moment and then nodded her head. "Jane. Yeah, I like that. Until I know the truth, call me Jane."

Camille noted that on her chart while Dr. Weston smiled warmly at her.

"Jane it is! Now, get some rest. I'll have the kitchen send up a meal for you. You need to eat," he said.

Then, he left with Camille close on his heels.

Looking around her room once more, Jane tried to put a positive spin on her situation. She did her best not to think about all the things she'd forgotten, instead focusing on the new things she could learn about herself.

She spoke aloud, staring at the heart monitor still beeping away, "Who are you, Jane?" She sighed. "I guess only time will tell."

THREE

Colt had just finished installing a new carburetor when his cell phone rang. He wiped his hands and pulled the black vibrating object out of his back pocket.

"Hello?"

"Hi, Colt. This is Monica from the hospital. I just wanted to let you know that your mystery girl is awake and seems to be doing well."

"Great. Thanks for letting me know." He paused. "I'm glad to hear she's okay."

"You're welcome." Monica's voice raised an octave as she said, "You know, she's in room one-oh-seven…just in case you want to check in on her."

Colt huffed out a small laugh. "Yeah. Okay."

"Well, it's totally up to you, but she might like the chance to thank her hero."

"I'm no one's hero, Monica."

"I'm sure she would beg to differ."

"Yeah, well…thanks again for calling."

"Bye, Colt."

He pressed the End button and stared at the phone. *Did he want to see her?* He wasn't sure. He admitted to himself that he was at least curious about her. If he were being totally honest with himself, he had to concede that she'd constantly been on his mind since he left her at the hospital. But he had no idea why he couldn't shake her from his thoughts. He never thought this much about the women he got involved with. *So, why is a complete stranger holding his attention hostage?*

He decided the best course of action to satisfy his curiosity would be to visit her. Then, he could get her out of his system and move on with his life. Colt just hoped she wasn't a melodramatic person. He wasn't the hero type, and he sincerely wanted to avoid an embarrassing display of mushy gratitude.

Putting away the rest of his tools, Colt locked up his toolbox and walked to Mike's office. Without knocking, he strolled in and leaned against a file cabinet.

"What's up, Colt?"

"I finished up that Road King, and I need to cut out early."

Mike raised an inquiring eyebrow. "Oh?"

Colt knew Mike was waiting for an explanation, but he didn't feel like giving one, so he just nodded his head.

Mike sighed. "May I ask, why do you need to leave now?"

Colt gave Mike a grim smile. "Yep, you can ask."

Mike looked at him for a moment longer. "But you aren't going to tell me, right?"

"You got it."

"Fine. Just be sure you come in early tomorrow."

Colt nodded, pushed himself away from the file cabinet, and left the office. After punching out his time card, he went to his locker and grabbed his keys.

Before he made it out the back door, Jerry called out to him. "Aw, does Colt need more time off to cope with losing his daddy?"

Colt turned on his heels and stared Jerry down. Then, he smiled. "Nope. Just off to do your mom, Jerry."

He turned and walked out of the shop, hearing Jerry screaming obscenities at him, and he closed the door just before Jerry threw something at it.

Colt's smile widened. Pissing off Jerry was becoming one of his favorite hobbies.

Thirty minutes later, Colt was showered and in clean clothes, and he walked through the double doors at the entrance of the hospital.

He located the first-floor patient rooms and searched for number *107*. He stood outside the door, trying to decide if he really wanted to go inside. He wasn't afraid or even nervous. Those were two emotions Colt rarely felt anymore. His hesitation stemmed from his concerns that this visit would only further his infatuation with her. He took a deep breath and knocked on the door.

From the other side, he heard a melodic soft voice say, "Come in."

He pushed the door open and walked into the partially sunlit room. He always hated hospitals, but somehow, this room felt less dreary. It was almost cheerful.

Colt looked at the woman sitting up in the bed. He could hardly believe his eyes. She barely resembled the dirt-covered sick girl he'd left there a week earlier.

Her straight auburn hair was freshly washed and hanging long down her back. Her face was clean, and there were only faint traces of the scrapes she'd obtained before she'd found his cabin. He could see that she'd also gained a little weight as her sunken cheeks had started filling out, and her skin was regaining color. She still looked young but not as young as he'd originally thought.

Jane looked up at the handsome stranger standing at the foot of her bed. She didn't know if she was supposed to know him, but he seemed friendly, so she gave him a shy smile. "Hi."

Colt cleared the sudden frog in this throat. Her smile had transformed her from a lovely young woman to something almost otherworldly. He was caught off guard. And her voice seemed to draw him in almost as much as her smile. After finding his own voice, he replied, "Hi. I'm Colt."

"Hi, Colt. I'm Jane."

They stared at one another for a few moments, and the silence became a little awkward.

She looked down at her fingers, nervously twitching them, and then she raised her eyes to his. "Colt, can I ask you a question?"

He moved to the chair beside her bed and took a seat. "Sure. Ask away."

"Are we friends? I mean, did we know each other before my accident?"

Colt was confused. *Why would she ask a question like that? She doesn't know if we know each other?* "No. We don't know each other. You don't remember your accident?"

Jane shook her head. "Unfortunately, I can't remember anything. The doctor thinks my memories may eventually come back, but for now, I'm a complete mystery to everyone, including myself."

Colt slowly nodded his understanding.

She eyed him cautiously. "If we don't know each other, why are you here?"

"Ah. I'm the one who brought you here. You knocked on my door and then passed out."

Jane's eyes grew wide. "So, you're the man I owe my life to."

Colt vigorously shook his head. This was exactly what he'd wanted to avoid. "No. You don't owe me anything. Just focus on getting better."

Jane smiled at him again. "Regardless, thank you. You could have just left me lying there."

17

"No. I just did what any other person would have done. It was nothing. Besides, it would have been a pain in the ass to step over you every time I walked through the door." Colt's teasing smirk assured her that he was only kidding about that last part.

She tried to contain a laugh.

He decided to change the subject. "So, you don't remember anything at all? I guess you remember your name at least."

"No, not even my name. I decided to use Jane because I'm a Jane Doe. Hopefully, my real name will come back to me at some point."

Colt sensed her apprehension and fear, despite her calm exterior. He could only imagine how frightening it would be to wake up in a strange place with no clue about your identity or past. He once again felt that pull to protect her.

He shook his head. "Man, sorry. That sucks."

She shrugged her shoulders. "It's just how it is, but yeah, it sucks." She managed another smile, this one less confident than before. "The good news is, the doctor says I'm healing amazingly well. At this rate, I can go home in a few days—well, not home. I don't know where that is. But he said I could stay at a woman's shelter until we figured something out."

Colt frowned at the thought of her staying in that dingy little shelter. It was an important resource to the community, but it was in dire need of some upgrades. Why it should matter to him, he had no clue, but it did matter.

Feeling slightly panicked at the turn his thoughts had taken, he abruptly stood. "I gotta go. I just wanted to see that you were okay. Glad you're feeling better."

He turned to leave when she said his name and stopped him in his tracks.

"Colt…thank you for coming to see me. It's nice to know that someone cares even if we are strangers."

His heart constricted. "We know each other's names, and we've had a conversation. As I see it, I think that's enough to make us friends." He gave her his most dazzling smile.

She smiled back at him, and he could see that his words had hit their mark. For at least a few minutes, she felt a little better. For some odd reason, that made him feel a little better, too.

"Thank you, Colt. I appreciate that very much. Would you mind coming back to see me tomorrow?"

I really shouldn't, Jane. You wouldn't benefit from knowing me. I'm bad news. "I wouldn't mind at all. I'll bring cards. Have you ever played poker?"

She let out a small chuckle. "I don't know. It doesn't sound familiar. I guess you'll have to teach me."

"I'd be honored to. There's nothing more rewarding than turning an innocent miss into a card shark."

"How do you know I'm so innocent? I might have been a very bad girl in my past life."

Colt tried not to let his thoughts wander in that direction. He had a great imagination, and he could easily envision her being a bad girl... with him.

She saw his odd expression and laughed out loud. He couldn't help but laugh with her.

"Poker sounds fun, Colt. See you tomorrow."

"See you then." He gave her a wink and left the room.

He was lost in thought as he exited the building and found his motorcycle. *What the hell just happened? I was supposed to meet her, end this weird fascination, and move on.*

He had a sinking feeling that this was going to be a lot more complicated than he had expected.

The next evening, true to his word, Colt spent some time teaching Jane how to play poker. Jane was a quick learner, and by the end of their fourth hand, she had actually won. She'd wagered her vanilla pudding against his black leather wrist cuff.

"Damn." Colt started to remove the cuff.

She laughed and placed a hand on his wrist. "No. Leave it on. I don't really want it."

"No way, lady. I always pay my debts. The cuff is yours."

She raised a skeptical eyebrow in his direction. "Did you really want my pudding?"

He grinned. "No, not really."

"It's all good then. I'd rather you answer a question for my prize anyway."

He shuffled the deck. "What question did you have in mind?"

Jane looked at his arms and then back at his face. "Do your tattoos mean anything?"

Colt froze mid shuffle. He didn't know what he'd expected her to ask, but that sure wasn't it.

He placed the deck on the table and moved his right bicep closer to her. "Some do. Some don't." He pointed to an American flag peeking out from beneath the sleeve of his T-shirt, and then he rolled the fabric up a bit, so she could get a better look. "This is my newest one. It's for my dad. He was a veteran. I lost him a few weeks ago."

"I'm so sorry. I didn't mean to intrude."

Colt sat back and smiled. "Nah. You aren't intruding. Dad was pretty great. He would've loved that you just kicked my ass in poker. He always said that we boys needed someone to knock us down a peg or two every now and then."

Jane hurt for his loss, but she gave him a smile. "It sounds like you had a good relationship with him."

He gazed at the flag with the name *Randy* just below it. "Yeah, I did."

She leaned forward to get a better look at the other tattoos on his arm, but Colt shook his head.

"One answer per winning hand." He smiled, a wicked gleam in his grayish-blue eyes. "Maybe when you get out of here, I can teach you a few other games. Strip poker can be very entertaining."

Jane's eyes grew wide, and for a few seconds, she was slightly shocked. Then, she started laughing so hard that she needed to wipe the tears from her eyes.

Colt ruffled a bit. "Why, may I ask, was that so funny?"

She sat back against her pillows and gave Colt a quick once-over. He was certainly a handsome man. He wore his neatly trimmed blond hair in a spiked style in the front. His eyes reminded her of storm clouds just before they'd break loose and dump their contents on the earth. He was tall and looked like he was a regular at the gym. Not to mention, he had an attitude of confidence that exuded sexiness. She could envision women falling all over themselves to get his attention.

"How many girls have you used that line on?" she asked.

He crossed his arms, a little annoyed that she'd laughed. "Not too many," he admitted.

"Does it ever actually work?"

He couldn't help but laugh. "So far, so good."

"Well, write today down on your calendar, mister, because that one just bombed."

Colt gave his chin a scratch as he studied her. "Well then, I guess I'll have to try harder with you."

He gave her a wink, and they both laughed again.

"It's getting late. I guess I'd better head home. Get some rest, Jane."

"Will you visit me again?"

Colt looked uneasy, and she worried that her only friend was already tired of her.

"I don't mean tomorrow. I just wondered if you might visit again soon. I need to practice if I'm gonna clean up in Vegas someday."

He nodded. "I'll try to stop back by before the weekend is up."

Colt had intended to keep himself occupied for the next several days with work and a few games of pool at his favorite bar, The Rusty Hinge. A distraction was always waiting for him there—usually in the form of a short skirt and cleavage-revealing top to go along with loose morals.

But every time he left for the bar, he'd end up in the hospital parking lot. It was almost as if he had no control over his actions. His brain said, *Bar*, but his body said, *Jane*.

He'd wind up in her room, playing poker and talking about a little bit of everything.

By the end of the week, he didn't even try to pretend that he was going to go out to party. He didn't understand why he was so drawn to the enigma that was Jane, but he did know that he honestly enjoyed spending time with her.

If he had to put a label on their relationship, he'd say they were friends, which was weird for him. It wasn't in his nature to be this attentive to anyone—with the exception of his little brother.

Colt walked into Jane's room to find her sitting up in bed with Dr. Weston situated in the chair next to her. She lifted her eyes to Colt's face and gave him a smile that he was sure could have lit up the darkest cavern in existence. It had been a long time since someone was genuinely happy to see him, and he felt her slip through one more chink in his armor.

"Hi, Colt! Dr. Weston was just telling me that I should be able to get out of here this weekend. Isn't that fantastic?"

Colt smiled back at Jane. "That is fantastic." He turned to Dr. Weston. "I don't wanna be a party pooper, but are you sure she's ready, Doc?"

"She's made a remarkable recovery, Colt. I'd call it almost miraculous." Dr. Weston looked at Jane and smiled as he pointed upward. "I think someone up there likes you, missy."

Jane laughed. "I hope you're right, Dr. Weston. I think I'm going to need that kind of favor in my life for a while."

Colt tried to be happy for her, but he worried about what her future would hold. She still had no recollection of her previous life.

How do you move on from that?

Dr. Weston started instructing Jane on her aftercare once she was discharged.

Colt stood back and observed. She did seem astonishingly well, especially considering she'd been on death's door and in the hospital for a little less than two weeks. Yet there she was with a pink hue in her cheeks and a sparkle in her emerald eyes. All traces of her injuries were completely gone. No one would ever accuse Colt of being a believer, but the sight before him certainly did seem like more of a miracle than a cure from medicine.

Dr. Weston rose from his chair. "Colt, could I talk to you for a moment?"

Colt nodded and followed him out the door, giving Jane an eye roll as he left. He heard her stifling a laugh before he shut the door behind him.

"Colt, I've made arrangements with Jessica Dorset for Jane. Jessica will pick Jane up tomorrow and help her get settled in the shelter. She's going to need a friend in the coming weeks, and I'm hoping you'll be that person."

"Me? Doc, I'm not exactly the nurturing Florence Nightingale type. I'm sure she'd be better off with someone else."

"That's just it, Colt. She has no one else. We've searched the Missing Persons Database and sent her pictures to several agencies. So far, no one has stepped up to claim her. You're the only friend she has right now, and she seems to trust you."

Colt sighed. "Why would she trust me? She barely knows me."

"Beats me, boy." Dr. Weston jabbed a finger in Colt's chest. "But she'd better not be wrong. Do I make myself clear?"

Colt didn't usually tolerate being threatened, but with Dr. Weston, he could only bite back his smile. "Yes, sir. I'll do my best not to disappoint."

"Glad to hear it. Now, get in there, so she can kick your butt in poker."

Colt gave Dr. Weston a nod, and then he turned and entered Jane's room. As he shut the door behind him, he heard Jane mumbling something, but he didn't quite catch it.

Once he approached the bed, he realized she was asleep.

She turned her head on the pillow and faced Colt. Her eyes peacefully closed, her long lashes rested on her lightly freckled skin. Then, she snuggled down into the covers and murmured a breathy, "Colt…"

The jolt of electricity Colt felt from just hearing her speak his name in her sleep made him realize that he was already in way over his head.

FOUR

Jane set a small duffel bag on her new bed. She glanced around the modest room and sighed. Today, she started her new life, and all her worldly possessions were waiting to be unpacked in her new home. Never mind that the new home was a tiny room in a women's shelter, and the aforementioned possessions amounted to a toothbrush, a hair brush, and a clean change of clothes, which had all been given to her by the kind nurse Camille.

Jane felt overwhelming gratitude to everyone who had helped her through this ordeal. Dr. Weston, Camille, and even Jessica—the administrator of the shelter—they'd been nothing but kind to her. Then, there was Colt. She had no idea how to describe what Colt meant to her, but she knew that he was meant to be in her life in one way or another.

She moved to the window and opened the blinds. Staring out at the small playground just a few feet from her window, she noticed two children playing. Jane smiled to herself as she watched them running and laughing. Her heart filled with joy. It was almost as if she could feel what they felt as they frolicked in the sunshine. She closed her eyes and tried to visualize the happiness. Behind her eyelids, she could see a rainbow of colors dancing and swaying. She gave herself over to this inner environment, and suddenly, she was surrounded by a rhythm that seemed to caress her. She felt like she was floating, and she loved the sensation.

Jane was lost in these emotions when she heard a knock coming from behind her. Her eyes flew open, and she turned to face the door. "Come in."

Colt opened the door and stepped inside. "Hi, Jane. I just wanted to stop by and see how you were settling in."

He looked around the tiny room, trying to hide his disappointment. She instinctively knew he didn't approve of her new lodgings, but she didn't understand why.

"Hey, Colt. I'm doing well. I have a bed, four walls, and a roof. It's more than I had when I woke up in the hospital a couple of weeks ago. Oh, and Camille gave me—" She stopped abruptly. Her duffel bag was no longer on the bed. "Wait…where did it go?"

"Where did what go?" Colt looked as confused as she felt.

"My bag. It was right here."

He stepped toward the bed and looked at the floor. Then, he bent down and picked up a small black bag. "You mean this one?"

Jane frowned. "Yeah, that's it. But why was it on the floor?"

Colt gave her a smirk. "It probably fell off." Then, he placed it back on the bed.

"Yeah, I guess." She wasn't convinced. She knew there was no way the bag had fallen off the bed on its own. She had placed it right in the middle of the mattress.

"Anyway…I thought I'd see if you needed anything. Or maybe you'd like to get some lunch? I know a great little barbeque place."

She smiled and nodded her head. "That sounds wonderful. It'd be nice to see a little bit of the town."

"Great. They just started the lunch special, so if we leave now, we can beat the crowd."

Jane grabbed her jacket from the foot of the bed and followed him out the door. But before she closed it, she gave her duffel bag one last glance.

Less than fifteen minutes later, they were seated in a corner booth at Smokey Bones BBQ.

Colt was looking at the menu, feeling a bit uncomfortable. The restaurant wasn't packed yet, but it would be soon, and people were already staring at them. Granted, it was probably more at her. He had to admit, she was a vision. Her hair was pulled back from her face with a clip, the rest falling gracefully around her shoulders. Her complexion was flawless, and she had just a small touch of pink lip gloss on her full lips. A smattering of light freckles crossed her nose and continued under both eyes, but it wasn't unattractive in the least. It seemed to add to her charm, not to mention her eyes—those same eyes that he would see in his sleep.

He shifted in his seat and tried to concentrate on lunch specials. Jane seemed to be engrossed in the menu as well.

When the waitress arrived to take their order, Jane nearly jumped out of her seat.

"Are you okay?" asked Colt. The concern in his voice was echoed by the look in his eyes.

"Yes. Yes, I'm fine. I'm not sure what came over me. I guess I'm still a little tired."

The waitress, whose name tag said *Bess*, gave Jane a skeptical glance, and then she turned her attention toward Colt. She leaned in close, and Colt got a good look at her cleavage, which he suspected was her intent. This wasn't anything new to him, and normally, he enjoyed the attention, but it only annoyed him this time.

"Hey, Colt. What can I get for you?"

"I'll take a large glass of water and the pulled pork sandwich."

Bess jotted his order down and gave him a sweet smile. Then, she turned to Jane, and her demeanor changed ever so slightly. It wasn't enough that most people would have caught it, but Jane did.

"So...what do you want?"

Jane peeked above the menu and looked at Bess. "I'd like a cobb salad and a water, please."

Bess scribbled on her order pad once more and then tucked it into her apron. "I'll be right back with those waters." She gave Colt one last longing look and walked away.

Jane glanced around the room. Her nerves suddenly felt stretched to their limits. The people, the noise, and all the activity surrounding them seemed completely foreign to her. She tightly gripped the menu and closed her eyes, willing the unwelcome panic to disappear. She was working on controlling her breathing when she heard Colt say her name. She opened her eyes to see him staring at her with a frown on his face.

"Are you okay? I've been trying to get your attention, but it was like you weren't even here."

She swallowed a lump in her throat. "Yeah, I'm okay. I guess I zoned out for a moment."

"A moment? Jane, Bess brought our food five minutes ago. You've been sitting there, mangling that menu for the better part of fifteen minutes."

Fifteen minutes? She didn't understand how that could possibly be true. She was just looking around, and then she closed her eyes for less than a minute. "Really? It was that long?"

"Yeah, pretty much." Colt leaned forward to observe her closer. "Maybe we should call Dr. Weston. I think he released you from the hospital too quickly."

Jane raised her hand to stop him. "No. No, I'm fine. I think I'm just tired. So much has happened, and my situation is a little overwhelming."

He didn't appear to believe her.

"If you say so." He picked up his sandwich and took a bite. "When we're done here, I'll take you back, so you can rest. You probably shouldn't push yourself for a while."

She looked down at her salad, struggling to find her appetite. "Thank you. I think a nap is a good idea."

They finished their meals in relative silence. Colt ate quickly while Jane picked at her salad, finally eating enough to lessen her guilt over no longer being hungry.

He seemed to sense that she wasn't up for conversation, so during the drive back to the shelter, he kept his commentary short and sweet, only occasionally pointing out a town landmark or popular eatery. He pulled his old truck up to the doors at the shelter, and then he jumped out and ran to her side to open the door for her.

"Thank you for lunch, Colt. I'm sorry I wasn't better company."

He gave her a reassuring smile. "You were fine. Go get some rest, and I'll see you soon."

She started to walk away but turned back to him. "Colt…"

He took a step forward, waiting for her to finish her sentence. Instead, she also took a step forward and then hugged him. He was caught off guard by the action, and he just stood there, frozen in place.

Jane let go of him and stepped back. "I'm sorry. I shouldn't have done that. It's just…I needed a hug."

Colt immediately started kicking himself for not hugging her back. *Friends hug, right?* It didn't mean they were an item or anything. He was just being paranoid, but he had to admit that he was once again treading into new territory.

"I'm sorry, Jane. You have to understand…I'm not good at this whole friendship thing."

She gave him a sad smile. "It's okay. Maybe you're just out of practice." Then, she turned away from him and entered the building.

Colt continued to look at the door as it closed behind her. "Yeah, kid. Maybe you're right."

Jane had been resting peacefully when she was awoken by a noise. She bolted upright in bed and tried to let her eyes adjust to the darkness. She reached over and turned on a small bedside lamp.

Climbing out of bed, she stood and surveyed the room to find the source of the noise, but nothing obvious stood out to her. Everything appeared to be in order. The only place she couldn't see in this tiny room was inside the closet.

As she moved toward it, she felt apprehension building up inside of her. She had no idea why she felt so afraid. It didn't make sense, yet her terror was very real. She forced herself to grip the doorknob, but her fingers were trembling so badly that she wasn't certain they would work properly. As her hand closed around the cold metal knob, her mind flashed back to a dark room with small windows.

She saw herself inside with her hand on the knob, struggling to get the door open. She banged on the wood panels and screamed at the top of her lungs, but no one seemed to hear her cries for help.

Then, she heard the voice of a girl behind her.

"It's no use. They won't let you out."

"What? Why are we locked in here?"

The girl was on a small cot, mostly hidden under the covers.

Jane couldn't get a good look at her. "Who are you?"

The girl pulled the blanket down just a bit, and Jane could see vivid green eyes staring back at her.

"That's what you have to figure out."

Jane shook herself out of her dreamlike state and realized she was still holding the closet doorknob in her hand. She had no idea what had just happened, but it scared her almost as much as opening the door.

Slowly, she turned the handle and opened the closet. To her relief, the closet was empty.

In fact, it was too empty. Looking down at the floor, she noticed that what few clothes she owned were in a pile but still on their hangers. One or two hangers were still hooked on the bar, swinging wildly.

Speaking out loud to only herself, she said, "What the…how did this happen?"

She carefully reached down and picked up each item, hanging it back in place in the closet.

Once that was done, she shut the door and returned to her bed. She tried to sleep, but it was not meant to be. When she closed her eyes, all she could see was a little girl on a cot, hiding under a blanket.

Colt had stopped by the shelter a couple of times since Jane moved in about a week ago. He was afraid if he stopped by daily, people would think they were an item.

Colt wasn't a commitment kind of guy, so he didn't want rumors to start. And he sure as hell didn't want Jane to get the wrong idea. Yet he found it difficult to stay away. In total honesty, he could admit that he was attracted to her, but he was drawing the line there. She didn't need a loner like him making her life worse. She deserved better.

Dr. Weston had mentioned to Colt that he guessed she was in her early twenties, so it wasn't like he would be breaking any laws if he were to hook up with Jane. At times though, she certainly seemed much younger, much more innocent than any twenty-something he'd ever met.

Regardless, he promised himself that he'd do the right thing for once in his life. His attraction for her would go no further than his mind, including the occasional vivid dream.

After a particularly crazy day at work, Colt was a bit on edge and needed a drink. He drove to The Rusty Hinge and found a seat at the bar.

He was downing his second beer and thinking about Jane when she suddenly seemed to materialize before his eyes. He put his beer on the bar and rose to his feet. Without even thinking, he walked toward her.

Jane was standing near the door with her newest friend Carol, a volunteer at the shelter. They were both decked out in form-fitting dresses that accentuated every curve. Jane's auburn tresses were coiled in a loose bun at the base of her neck with stray tendrils falling near her temples. At five-seven, she was taller than most of the women there, but she was still shorter than Colt's six-one stature.

In his eyes, she looked like a goddess.

As he approached, Jane's eyes widened with surprise.

"Hello, ladies. Can I buy you a drink?"

Carol blushed, but she was thrilled that the notorious Colt Henderson was paying attention to them even if it was mostly for Jane's benefit. He was considered to be quite a catch by most of the single ladies within a fifty-mile radius. The problem was keeping him once you'd caught him because he never stayed put long. Carol secretly wondered if Jane would be the one to achieve the impossible.

Colt walked the ladies to the bar, one hand on the small of each of their backs. "Anything you want, it's on me."

Carol turned to Colt. "That's very nice of you. Thanks!" Then, she addressed the bartender and ordered a gin and tonic.

Jane had no idea what to order. She didn't even know if she liked alcohol. Carol had suggested this whole girls' night out, but Jane had her reservations. Dr. Weston had seemed positive that she was at or above legal drinking age, but since she didn't have any ID, she hadn't even been sure that they'd let her in.

Carol had loaned Jane the clothes and worked some magic with her makeup and hair. Then, suddenly, she no longer looked like a teenager. Carol had remarked that Jane was stunning and would easily leave the bar with a date, but that didn't really appeal to Jane. If she wanted to impress anyone, it would be Colt, but she hadn't expected to run into him.

Yet there he was with his hand possessively planted on her back, offering to buy her a drink. She felt a small sliver of happiness rise in her chest.

Jane looked at all the various liquor bottles lining the wall behind the bar and shook her head. "I have no idea what to order."

Colt smiled at her. "Let's start you off with something easy. You like cola, right?"

She nodded her head. "Yes, I do."

"Great. You'll like this then." He turned toward the bartender. "James, rum and Coke for the little gal here."

James poured her drink and passed it across the bar. "There ya go, miss. Anything else I can get for you?"

He flashed her a smile, and she got the impression that he might be flirting a little.

Colt paid James for the drink and gave him a glare. "She's good for now."

Jane took a sip of the rum and Coke, and she was pleasantly surprised. "Wow! That's really good!"

Colt couldn't help but chuckle at her enthusiasm for something so small. That was one thing about Jane that had drawn him in. She had all these obstacles to overcome, yet each new discovery would bring her joy, and that joy was infectious.

Carol had already found someone to dance with, and she was out on the floor, leaving her mostly empty glass behind. Colt directed Jane to a small table near the back, and then he ordered another round from a passing server. Jane was just finishing up her drink when the second one arrived. She handed her empty glass to the waitress and smiled as she took a gulp of the next one.

"Whoa, slow down there. If you aren't accustomed to alcohol, you don't want to overdo it," Colt warned.

"Oh, right." Jane was a little embarrassed. She didn't want him to think she was a lush or something. She just really liked that drink combination.

Colt turned out to be very right. Before the hour was up, she'd finished her third rum and Coke, and she was feeling a little light-headed. She excused herself to go to the ladies' room, located near the pool tables in the back, and then she carefully made her way to the correct door.

At least, she thought it was the correct door.

When she pushed open the door and stumbled in, a large man was standing at a urinal, just zipping his fly. He turned to her and smiled.

"Oh, I'm so very sorry. I thought this was the ladies' room."

"No problem, baby. You don't need the ladies' room. I'm happy to share."

He took a few steps closer, and she realized he reeked of beer and cigarettes. Despite being buzzed, she knew that this was not a good situation, so she took a step back, coming up against the closed door. As she turned to pull the handle, the man grabbed her and put his hand over her mouth.

"No need to scream or struggle. I promise, you'll enjoy this," he said.

He pulled her to the other side of the restroom while she kicked at his shins. He pushed her against the wall, and she panicked. She couldn't get free, and fear took over her entire being. Closing her eyes, she saw a swirling black mass continually changing shapes behind her eyelids.

When she felt him touch her breast, she screamed internally. At the same time, the full wall-length mirror and two small windows in the restroom shattered into thousands of tiny shards, flying around them as if swept up in a whirlwind. The man shouted as glass embedded itself into his back, and he let go of her, ducking to the floor as he covered his head.

Jane opened her eyes to see him cowering in front of her, blood running down his skin in various places. The floor was littered with sharp fragments, and other pieces were stuck in the wall, but she was completely unharmed.

Colt knew Jane had had a little too much to drink, so he decided to check on her. He pushed the door open to the women's restroom and looked around. When he realized she wasn't in there, he was confused. Then, he heard a commotion coming from the men's room, and he went in to check it out.

The man Colt knew as Max uncovered his head and looked around the room, clearly in shock.

He glanced warily at Jane as he stood up. He then turned to Colt and pointed at her. "She's a witch or something! She made this happen!"

Colt strolled inside, kicking aside glass as he walked. He noticed Jane was visibly shaken. "She's not a witch. But you're a drunk and an idiot. Get out of here before I kill you myself." As Max scooted past him, Colt grabbed his shirt and stared him in the eyes. "If you ever tell anyone that she's anything other than a lady, I'll hunt you down and gut you like a fish. Got it?"

Max crossed his chest with his index finger. "Whatever you say, Colt. I swear!"

Colt let go of his shirt, and Max scampered out of the room as quickly as possible. Jane was still up against the back wall, and Colt could see she was still scared.

"It's okay, sweetheart. I'm here. You're safe."

She blinked for a moment, as if she was trying to determine if he was real or a mirage, and then she ran to him.

He wrapped his arms around her. "Let's get out of here."

He led her to the bar and paid their tab. While he waited for his change, he motioned for Carol to join them.

As she approached, she noticed that Jane was upset. "What happened?"

"She had a little run-in with a drunk. I'm gonna take her home."

Carol hugged Jane. "I'm sorry, honey. I'll be around tomorrow if you want to talk."

Jane gave Carol a sad smile. "Thanks."

Colt pocketed his wallet and grabbed Jane's hand. Once out in the parking lot, he found his motorcycle and handed her the helmet. "Here, put this on."

As she strapped on the helmet, Colt started the bike and gestured for her to climb on. Jane crawled up behind him and wrapped her arms around his waist, clinging to him as if her life depended on it. She didn't have a clue as to what had just happened in the bar, but it scared the hell out of her to think she might have been the cause.

FIVE

Colt pulled his bike into the garage attached to his small two-bedroom home and shut off the ignition. Jane carefully slid off the side, and then he followed, taking the helmet from her to put it away.

Looking down at her, he could see that she still seemed shaken from the incident at the bar. He put his hands on her shoulders. "Hey, are you okay, sweetheart?"

Jane looked up to his face, tears resting on the edges of her lashes. "I will be. I'm just…confused."

Colt pulled her in for a hug. "I know. We'll figure all this out together, okay? I promise."

She attempted a weak smile. "Thank you, Colt. I don't know what I'd do without you."

He gave her another squeeze and they both entered the house. He froze when he heard his stereo click on, blaring Metallica. He turned to Jane. "It's okay. It's just my brother, Brett. He must be home for the weekend."

Walking into the kitchen, he tossed his keys into a bowl, and then he grasped Jane's hand and led her into the living room. Colt's twenty-one-year-old brother was sitting on the couch, sipping a beer and looking surly. It was exactly what Colt had expected to see. Brett only listened to metal when he was in a pissy mood—usually after a breakup.

Brett looked up, and his eyes went wide. He jumped to his feet and hit the remote, turning off the music. "Colt! Sorry to barge in! I just thought I'd stop by and see what you were doing. It looks like you're busy, so I can come back later."

Colt knew Brett thought he was bringing home his latest one-night stand, but he felt compelled to correct his brother. He couldn't stand the thought of anyone thinking badly of Jane. "No, it's fine, Brett. I was hoping to introduce you two anyway." He turned to face Jane. "Jane, meet my brother, Brett." Then, he faced his brother. "Brett, this is Jane."

Brett seemed to choke for a moment. "*This* is Jane?" He looked her over once more. "Holy sh—"

Colt held up a hand, interrupting that thought. "Not in front of the lady, Brett."

"Oh, yeah. Sorry, Jane. It's very nice to meet you. I've heard a lot about you from Colt."

Jane seemed surprised by that admission. "It's nice to meet you, too, Brett."

"Would you like a drink? I just put some beer in the fridge."

"No, thanks. I've had enough tonight."

"Oh. Well, I think Colt has some tea or orange juice in there, too."

Jane gave Brett one of her genuine smiles, the kind that made Colt's heart skip a beat. He suddenly found himself wanting to smack his little brother. Colt had no idea what hold this woman had on him, but it seemed to be wrapping around him like a noose. To be honest though, he wasn't sure if he wanted to escape it.

Jane clasped her hands behind her back as she cleared her throat. "Some juice would be nice."

Brett nodded and practically ran into the kitchen.

Colt rolled his eyes. He motioned to the couch and waited for her to take a seat, and then he sat beside her. He took one of her delicate hands in his and gave it a slight squeeze. "We'll talk whenever you're ready. No pressure, okay?"

She simply nodded.

Brett entered the room with a glass of orange juice and handed it to Jane. She took a sip and then placed the glass on the coffee table, her hand shaking slightly.

Noticing that small detail, Brett gave Colt a knowing look that said, *I see you need alone time.* "Well, I think I'm gonna hit the hay. It's been a long day. Good night, Colt. Hope to see you again soon, Jane."

"Good night," Jane and Colt said in unison.

Once Brett had shut the bedroom door, Colt turned to Jane. He watched her take another sip of her juice as she closed her eyes. When she opened them, she seemed to have some of her resolve back, but he could still sense the underlying fear, too.

She took a deep breath. "Colt, I don't know what happened."

He tried to keep his anger in check. He wanted to kill Max for scaring her. And if Max had touched her at all, Colt planned on killing the man slowly.

"Did he hurt you? Did he..." Colt struggled to say it out loud. The idea of Max touching her in any way made his temper rise.

"No! I mean, not really. I think he would have hurt me, but then…it happened."

"It? You mean, the glass?"

She nodded, placing the juice back on the table. "I don't know, Colt. I was so scared. I couldn't get away. I closed my eyes and felt an intense fear that I could almost see in my mind. The next thing I knew, glass was exploding everywhere."

Colt frowned. "That is kinda odd, but I'm sure there's an explanation of some kind. Maybe a minor earthquake?"

"In one room?"

"Yeah, that doesn't make sense. Could have been the building shifting or a strong wind?"

They both knew he was grasping at straws.

"I don't know. But other things have happened, too, Colt."

"Like what?"

Jane reminded him about the bag and then told him about the closet and her strange vision.

Colt had no idea how to respond to that. It sounded like something right out of a science-fiction movie. And he sure as hell wasn't a scientist, so he couldn't explain it even if there were a reasonable explanation.

Jane leaned back and blew out a puff of breath, causing a tendril of red hair to flutter away from her face before landing over one eye. Without thinking, Colt reached over and tucked it behind her ear. She looked into his eyes and felt a tiny flutter in her chest. She was warm and tingly, and she was sure he was going to kiss her. She gave him a shy smile and closed her eyes as she leaned forward ever so slightly.

Colt almost responded in turn, but at the last minute, he stopped himself. *What am I doing?* He really liked Jane. He didn't want to mess up their friendship, and he knew a kiss would be the beginning of the end. Besides, he had convinced himself that she was like a little sister he needed to protect. Currently, he wasn't having little-sister thoughts about her, and that frustrated him.

He sat back and cleared his throat.

Jane opened her eyes, and her cheeks reddened with embarrassment, which was easily obvious on her porcelain skin. He inwardly groaned. He felt bad that he hadn't kissed her, but he knew he would have felt bad if he had. There was no way to win.

"Jane, I don't know what is happening to you, but I'll be here to help you through it. I hope you believe that."

"I do, Colt. Thank you."

"Listen, if you're okay with staying here, you can have my room, and I'll sleep on the couch. I'm not sure you should be alone right now."

"I'd appreciate that very much. I don't feel like being alone."

Colt stood. "Great. I'll go get some fresh sheets to put on the bed. I'll be right back."

While Colt was in the bedroom, Jane strolled around the living room, looking at family photos and smiling. There were several of Colt and Brett as boys, playing in the mud or proudly standing next to their bicycles. She also noticed a man who had to be their father. The men looked very much like him with only minor differences.

She wondered what her own father looked like. *Did she resemble him at all?* It made her sad to know she might never remember her parents. She glanced at a collection of photos on another bookshelf and quickly realized there were no women in the pictures.

Did their mother hate getting her picture taken?

"No. She left my dad when Brett was barely a year old, so we don't have any photos with her."

Jane felt her cheeks redden once again. She hadn't realized she'd asked the question out loud. "I'm sorry about your mom. I can't imagine what that must have been like."

Colt shrugged. "It wasn't easy, but we managed. I don't know what it's like to have amnesia either, so we're even." He gave her a smile and a wink, trying to put her at ease.

It wasn't a topic he liked to talk about. He remembered his mother, but Brett had been too young to develop those maternal memories that would hit him like a knife to the chest. Colt was thankful for small favors. He knew Brett felt the loss as well, but there was something about knowing things—how her voice had sounded, how her arms had felt, how she'd smelled—that made her leaving them feel like an intense betrayal.

His dad had simply told him, "That's how women are, son. Just enjoy your time with them for a while, but don't fall in love. None of them ever stay long, and it's not worth the heartbreak."

Colt had taken that to heart while Brett was the exact opposite, planning to marry every girl he dated. It'd drive Colt crazy that Brett couldn't see that most relationships had been built on shallow, selfish needs. Once those needs were filled, you'd move on. Sure, a few people seemed to make it work for life, but Colt didn't believe that was the norm.

Jane yawned, shaking Colt out of his thoughts.

"Sorry, uh...your room is ready." He walked down the narrow hallway with Jane following right behind him, and he opened a door to the left. "You can sleep here. Brett's room is across the hall, but don't worry. He won't bother you." He pointed to the door at the end of the hall, positioned between the two bedrooms. "That's the bathroom. Feel free to make yourself at home." He reached into a closet off to the side and pulled out a blanket and a pillow. "I'll be on the couch if you need me."

"Thank you again, Colt. I feel bad that you are giving up your bed."

"Don't feel bad. I'm glad to do it. Get some rest." He leaned forward and kissed her forehead. "Good night."

"Good night, Colt."

Somewhere around two a.m., Colt was still tossing and turning, trying to get comfortable. His large frame didn't fit well on the small couch. He could feel how lumpy the cushions had become, and he was pretty sure he felt a broken spring in there somewhere. He made a mental note to buy a new couch with his next tax refund.

He had just rolled over for the umpteenth time when he heard a crash coming from one of the bedrooms. He bolted up and ran down the hallway. Just as he opened the door, something else crashed inside the room.

He flipped on the light to see Jane asleep, tossing her head back and forth in the midst of what appeared to be a nightmare. On the floor, he found the remains of a drinking glass. The wall showed evidence of where it had hit and broken. Water ran down the blue paint, making light shiny streaks.

He didn't see the item that had caused the second noise. When Jane started to thrash faster, her legs moving as if she were running, he noticed movement out of the corner of his eye. A frame rose into the air and started spinning slowly before gaining momentum. Colt couldn't believe his eyes. He ducked down just in time, the frame narrowly missing his head before hitting the open door beside him.

Jane still slept fitfully, none of the noises awaking her from her dream.

Colt dashed to the bed and tried to gently wake her.

She moaned. "No! No! Don't take me in there! It's scary! I promise, I'll be good!"

Not knowing how to help her, he pulled her to him and held her tight. "Jane, sweetheart, it's Colt. I'm here. You're safe with me. I won't let them take you."

He tried to stroke her face while still keeping her still as he murmured in her ear, "I'm here, Jane. I'm here. I'll always be here." Then, he kissed her cheek.

Her breathing began to slow, and her movements stopped. Her cheeks were wet from tears, and she still had a frown on her lovely face. Colt loosened his grip and ran a finger across her lips. She relaxed a little more. Then, he gently lowered his face to hers and kissed her. It was a kiss full of tenderness and concern. She went limp in his arms as she sighed, and then she snuggled into his shoulder.

Colt spent the rest of the night with Jane in his arms. Sleep that night would never come to him now, not after what he'd just witnessed. While it certainly freaked him out, he also felt more protective of her than ever.

Somewhere deep inside her subconscious, Jane remembered horrible things. She also had some kind of power that she didn't realize she possessed. She was on her own, and she'd need him to stick with her while she figured it all out. He could do that. He was sure he could. It wouldn't be easy, but Colt was determined to help her unlock and banish her demons.

Jane woke up the next morning to the smell of bacon frying. She stretched her arms and legs and then settled back into her pillow, looking up at the ceiling. She had the odd sensation that she hadn't been alone last night, but she didn't understand why. She reached over next to her and felt the empty space on the bed. She got the impression that Colt had been there.

She closed her eyes and thought of him. Once again, she saw small sparks of color behind her eyelids. They swirled and danced and then formed waves that seemed to crash over her. With each crash, she felt warmth and happiness. It felt like...love. She wasn't sure she knew what love even felt like, but she guessed it would have to be very close to this. If it didn't feel the same, it certainly should.

She smiled and opened her eyes. Then, she promptly dropped about a foot, landing on the bed with loud protests from the old springs.

She sat up in shock. *Was I just levitating? How is that possible?*

She was still sitting upright in bed, lost in her thoughts, when Colt knocked on the door.

He entered, carrying a tray with eggs, bacon, toast, and orange juice. "How are you feeling?"

She tried to smile, still a little stunned from her earlier revelation. "I'm fine. You?"

Colt smiled. "Great. Slept like a rock."

His eyes said otherwise, but Jane didn't feel it was polite to point out his lie.

She scooted herself up the bed and sat against the headboard, so he could place the tray in front of her.

He tried to keep his eyes on the tray, but he couldn't help but notice the flash of her bare thigh peeking out from beneath the sheet. Since she only had the dress she'd worn to the bar, he'd given her one of his T-shirts to sleep in. Right now, it was his favorite shirt.

He mentally slapped himself and stepped back. "How did you sleep?"

His question was normal enough, but the way he'd said it made her suspect that he knew exactly how she'd slept.

Taking a bite of her toast, she studied him. Then, she placed it back on the plate and crossed her arms. "Okay, what's up?"

Colt tried to suppress a grin. It seemed she'd regained some of her spunk. "Nothing. Why do you ask?"

"Really, Colt, I can tell when you aren't being honest with me. Something happened."

He glanced around the room. After rising for the day, he'd cleaned up all the evidence of the destruction, but he could still see the impossible event in his mind. For once, he was thankful that Brett slept with earplugs. Colt couldn't imagine explaining this to his brother.

Jane tapped her fingers on the tray, waiting.

He sat on the bed and tried to give his voice a nonchalant tone as he said, "Well, you did have a bad dream last night. Do you remember it?"

She shook her head. "No, not really. I kind of remember feeling upset though." She frowned. She didn't understand why she could remember the feeling but not the dream.

"Oh, you were absolutely upset."

Her eyes snapped to his. "What did I do?" Her voice had a slight tremor that belied her calm exterior.

"Eat breakfast, sweetheart. You need your strength. Then, we'll talk."

She forced herself to eat, instinctively knowing that he was right about her needing strength. She feared the conversation that awaited them. There were things about herself that she wasn't sure she wanted to know.

SIX

Jane had finished her breakfast and was in the kitchen, helping Colt clean up. She was standing at the sink, washing dishes, still wearing his T-shirt. It covered her almost as much as the dress she'd worn last night, but this was infinitely sexier.

Jane was talking to Colt, but he was struggling to concentrate. His eyes kept wandering down her torso to her bare legs. Once he got there, his mind would wander further. While she was talking about finding jobs and getting an apartment, he was thinking of picking her up, so she could wrap those long legs around him while he set her on the counter.

"Colt? Colt!"

He blinked at her.

"Have you heard a word I've said?"

"Yeah. You're thinking about getting an apartment."

She placed her hands on her hips and sighed. That did nothing to help his concentration. The motion pulled the shirt tighter and allowed him to see more of her curves.

"That was ten minutes ago. I just asked you if we could talk about last night."

He rubbed a hand over his face and then up through his hair. "Yeah. We should do that."

He glanced at her legs once more and decided the only way they'd have a decent conversation was if she got dressed. Even that would be pushing it because he'd still have to fight off his mental images.

"Let me get you some sweatpants or something."

He rushed off to his room and grabbed a pair from his dresser. She'd have to roll them up and cinch up the waist, but at least she'd be covered.

He jogged back into the living room to find Jane sitting on the sofa, one leg crossed over the other.

He swallowed hard. "Here you go. That should keep you warm until you're ready to change back into your dress."

She smiled. "Thanks. That's very thoughtful of you."

He had to bite back a laugh. *No. Thoughtful has little to do with it. This is self-preservation, sweetheart.* "You're welcome."

She stood and placed her feet inside the waistband, and he turned around to give her privacy. She was innocent and probably had no idea what all this was doing to him. Sadly, that seemed to turn him on even more.

He could no longer admit that he was just being brotherly. He was intensely attracted to her, but if he acted on it, he'd eventually hurt her. He couldn't let that happen. She was different than the women he knew—in more ways than one. And he needed to discuss that with her.

They both sat on the couch.

Colt placed an arm behind her. "Jane, last night, you had a nightmare. You were thrashing on the bed, saying something about being scared."

Jane frowned and tried to remember.

He continued, "But that wasn't the weird part. The more upset you got, the more…" He wasn't sure how to say it. "Well, things were flying around the room. I was able to calm you, and when you finally relaxed, the chaos stopped."

Her eyes were wide, and her voice came out in a small squeak as she said, "Colt…what's wrong with me?"

He could see the fear on her face. He pulled her to him, hugging her. "I don't know, Jane. But I promised you that I'd help, and I never go back on a promise."

She pulled back and looked up to his face, tears on her cheeks. "But…when you promised, you didn't know I was…"

"Special?" he asked.

"No…a freak."

He shook his head. "What you are is amazing. It's overwhelming right now, but we'll figure it out."

Jane tried to smile and believe that Colt was right.

When he used one of his thumbs to wipe away her tears, she felt that warm wave rushing over her again. This time, she smiled for real.

Later that afternoon, Jane was back in her room at the shelter, dressed in jeans and a T-shirt, looking at the want ads in the newspaper.

Shortly after Jane had gotten back, Carol had stopped by to see how she was feeling. Jane had kept her explanation of the night before very vague, leaving out the bits about flying glass and bad dreams.

Colt had promised to take Jane to dinner after he ran some errands, so while she waited, she was searching for possible job opportunities. She couldn't brag about a lot of skills or past experience, so that was going to make it difficult to get a job. She didn't even have a Social Security number at this point.

She wadded the paper up in a ball and tossed it into a metal waste bin near her bed. Then, she angrily stared at it, the frustration of her entire situation building inside her. In one blinding moment, the newspaper went from a mangled ball to a small inferno. She jumped from the bed and tried to think of a way to put it out before the fire alarms sounded.

She didn't think fast enough. The alarm and sprinkler system went off at the same time, quickly drenching everything. Instead of exiting the building like everyone else, she stayed put and cried. The despair seemed to swallow her. She wondered if she could make herself disappear. She hoped that if she thought about it hard enough, she could just turn herself to ash and blow away in the wind. She was sure the whole world would be better off without her. So, she sat on the bed and let the sadness continue to wrap around her, focusing on the shades of gray and brown behind her eyelids.

To her humiliation, this was how the firemen found her—sitting on her bed with her eyes closed as if she were meditating while the sprinklers completely soaked her. They carried her out to the EMTs and wrapped her in a blanket. Everyone was staring at her.

She was starting to feel paranoid. *Do they know it was my fault? Do they know I started the fire?*

Shortly after, Colt pulled up in his truck. He noticed the emergency vehicles and leaped out of the driver's seat, frantically looking around. Then, he spotted her. He jogged over to the ambulance. Just his luck, Lance was on duty. He was talking to Jane and rubbing her arms covered with the blanket. Colt instantly wanted to hit him. Usually, Lance had to open his mouth and let a few words fall out before Colt would be prepped for a fight. But seeing Lance touching Jane was more than enough to set off Colt's ire.

Jane looked up. "Colt!" Her cheeks blushed a bright pink, and she looked down at her hands.

He immediately wondered if she was embarrassed that he'd caught her talking to Lance. *Does she like him? Well, that'd be Karma coming back to roost.*

During their senior year, Colt had been guilty of stealing a few girls away from Lance. Colt hadn't tried to make it happen. It just had, and Lance had hated him ever since.

Colt tried to clear the disturbing thought of Jane and Lance as a couple. "Are you okay? What happened here?"

Lance didn't give her a chance to answer. "Little fire. No big deal. I'm taking care of her."

Colt heard the challenge in Lance's words. He was staking his claim. But Colt could never resist a challenge, and when it came to Jane, he wasn't about to let Lance win.

"I'm glad you could help, Lance. I'll take it from here."

Lance clenched his fists. "I need to finish my examination and make sure she doesn't need further medical assistance."

Colt took a step forward and looked down at him. Lance stood his ground.

Jane watched them and was completely confused about what she was witnessing. "I'm fine. Really. I'm just wet...and a little embarrassed."

Colt took the two short steps needed to reach her, and then pulled her up and to him. "Are you really okay?" The concern in his eyes was evident.

"Yes. I'm really okay."

He breathed out a sigh of relief and then kissed the top of her head.

She stepped back and wrapped the blanket around her tightly. "Thank you for your help, Lance. I should get changed, so Colt and I can go."

Lance looked temporarily defeated, but then his determination returned. "Call me if you need me. Anytime, Jane. I mean it."

Colt moved toward Lance, but Jane stood between them.

She placed a hand on Lance's arm. "Thank you, Lance. I appreciate that." She gave him a smile and turned toward Colt. "Can we go now?"

He glared at Lance over the top of her head as he nodded. "Sure. My truck is over here."

She handed the blanket back to Lance and walked away with Colt. "I would get some dry clothes, but I'm not sure I have any now."

"I can take you to my house. You can wear my sweats again while we toss your clothes in the dryer."

She thought that was a good idea, and they started to walk to the truck when Mrs. Jameson—another of the shelter administrators—came running up to them with a stern frown on her face.

"Miss Jane! I must talk to you now!"

Jane turned. "Oh, hello, Mrs. Jameson. How can I help you?"

The elderly woman's brown wig bobbed as she shook her head. "I was just informed by a fireman that the blaze started in your room!"

Jane gave a sideways glance at Colt. "Uh...yes, in fact, it did. But it wasn't really a blaze. It was—"

"You know smoking is not allowed in the building!"

"Oh no! I wasn't smoking! I just...it was..."

How do I tell this woman I got angry and started a fire with my mind?

Jane still couldn't believe it herself, so there was no way anyone else would.

"I'm sorry, young lady, but we have very strict rules, and you've broken one. You'll have to find a new place to stay. You can pick up your belongings after this mess you've caused has been cleared up." Then, Mrs. Jameson turned on her heel and stomped off.

Jane stood there, dejected, as Colt made a growling noise and yelled at the retreating woman's backside, "Hateful old bat!"

Mrs. Jameson stopped for just a moment, and then she gave a subtle adjustment to her wig before continuing on as if she hadn't heard him.

Jane and Colt looked at each other and then burst out laughing.

Back at Colt's place, Jane changed into another one of his T-shirts and sweats. She tossed her clothes in the dryer while Colt ordered in a pizza. She made herself comfortable on the couch, and Colt turned on the TV. They sat in silence, watching the news, until the pizza arrived. Colt brought the pizza, napkins, plates, and sodas into the living room and laid it all out on the coffee table.

Jane was still looking at the screen, but she didn't seem to really be watching anything. She appeared lost in thought instead. Colt placed a hand over hers, and she blinked as she turned to look at him.

"You okay?"

She nodded. "Yes. I'm just really confused." She let out a big sigh. "It was bad enough when I didn't know who I was or where I belonged. But now…now, it feels like I don't even belong on this planet, let alone in this town. I'm scared, Colt. I'm not sure what I'm capable of or if I can control it, whatever it is."

He gave her hand a squeeze. "Maybe we can find someone to help. There has to be someone who knows something about this kind of thing."

She shrugged. "Maybe." Then, she closed her eyes and leaned her head back against the sofa. "I was upset, Colt. That's all it was. I was frustrated after looking through the newspaper. I never meant to set it on fire. I never meant any of what happened. What if I'm dangerous? What if I accidentally hurt someone?" she shared her concerns, her voice cracking.

He couldn't answer her. He didn't have any idea about what was going on, but oddly enough, she didn't scare him. He should have been totally freaked out by what he'd witnessed, yet he wasn't. Deep down, he felt sure she wasn't dangerous, and he believed Dr. Weston knew more than he'd let on when he said she was a miracle.

"Wait. What if we talked to Dr. Weston? He might have some explanation or at least know who we could talk to. I believe we can trust him."

Jane looked hopeful. "Do you really think so?"

Colt smiled at her. "Yeah. I really think so." He hugged her. "We'll call him tomorrow. Until we figure something else out, you can stay here. We have the spare bedroom that Brett only uses on his rare visits home, so you're welcome to it for as long as you need it."

Jane sighed, once again feeling the embarrassment of the earlier fiasco and her subsequent ejection from the shelter. She nodded and tried to relax, placing her head on his shoulder.

Colt needed to let her go, but he couldn't bring himself to do it. Instead, he leaned back and pulled her with him. She willingly followed him. He shifted again until they were lying on the couch together with her body snuggled comfortably on top of him. He stroked her hair, and she seemed to relax even more.

"Colt?"

"Yeah, sweetheart?"

"Thank you."

"For what?"

"For not running away from me, for making me feel like I'm not alone, for not thinking I'm some freak to be feared. When I'm with you, I feel safe."

He smiled as he continued to brush his fingers over her soft long tresses. "Believe me, it's my pleasure."

Two hours later, Jane woke up to find herself still wrapped in Colt's arms. The pizza and sodas sat on the coffee table, completely forgotten. His deep breathing told her that he was asleep.

She turned her head, so she could look at him, and then she rested her cheek back on his chest. She smiled as his chest rose and fell. She could almost hear his heartbeat, and she wondered what Colt dreamed about. He never talked about his future or what made him happy. He seemed to only live for the moment. She supposed that was a good thing. It was realistic with little chance of disappointment. *But didn't everyone have some kind of hopes and wishes for their lives?*

She closed her eyes and focused on his breathing, letting the feel of him seep into her mind and heart. She started seeing the familiar swirls of bright colors as joy washed over her. She snuggled in as close as she could to him.

Colt made a little moan and then tightened his arms around her. His lips parted, and he whispered her name. She looked up, and he blinked his eyes open and gazed at her. She smiled, and he gave her one in return. Something about the look in his eyes made her heart stop. It was like he could feel what she felt—the warmth and happiness. The idea that she might be able to make him feel her feelings startled her, and she quickly sat up.

Colt sat up as well, and then he yawned and stretched. "Are you okay?"

"Yes. I just realized how late it was. We should go to bed."

He gave her a sultry smile, and she had to try to calm her heart rate.

"I mean, we should probably get some sleep."

"We were just sleeping." He looked at the pizza. "And we forgot to eat."

She nodded. "Yeah, we did. I'm not really hungry now, so I'm gonna slip off to bed."

Colt watched her for a moment, trying to understand her sudden need to get away from him. "Sure. I'll get the sheets for the bed." He stood up and walked into Brett's room, shutting the door behind him.

Jane busied herself with cleaning up the coffee table and putting the soda and pizza into the fridge.

When Colt reappeared, he looked frustrated. "The bed's made, and I threw an extra blanket on there in case you needed it."

"Thanks." It seemed like such an inadequate word for all he'd done for her, yet at this time, it was all she had to offer.

"Yeah, well, I'm gonna hit the hay. Let me know if you need anything else."

She nodded and tried to smile. He continued to look at her as if he was expecting something. She swallowed and attempted to make her smile more convincing.

Colt crossed his arms. "Did I do something? Did I talk in my sleep or something?"

"Oh, goodness no!" She didn't know how to explain the panic she was feeling. "I think everything is hitting me at once. I'm feeling…broken."

He continued to stare at her, but his features softened a bit. "Well, you know where to find me."

She nodded again.

He walked back down the hall. When he reached his room, he turned to give her one last look. "Good night, Jane."

"Good night, Colt."

He shut the door behind him, and she blew out a nervous breath. She cared for him. She knew that without a doubt. *But what did he feel for her? And what if any feelings he did have weren't real because she was somehow manipulating them?*

Jane had no real clue what she was capable of, and the thought terrified and saddened her. She sincerely hoped Dr. Weston could help them find answers. She wasn't sure how long she could continue to second-guess every aspect of her existence before it drove her crazy.

SEVEN

ANGELS AND DEMONS ON EITHER SIDE,

I KNOW NOT WHERE TO TURN.

Jane sat in Dr. Weston's office, nervously fidgeting with a slip of paper the nurse had handed her.

It'd been eight days since the incident on Colt's couch. Since then, Dr. Weston had run a long list of tests and promised he'd keep her abilities a secret. Colt had been supportive and helpful as always, even stopping by the shelter to pick up the rest of her things, but there was an awkwardness between them that hadn't existed before. She knew it was her fault, and it would be up to her to fix it, but she wasn't exactly sure how. She didn't want to care for him too deeply, especially when she couldn't trust any perception of how he felt about her.

Dr. Weston entered the room as he flipped through the various pages in his hand. He sat down behind the desk and smiled up at her. "Jane, dear, I'll admit to believing you were unique when I first met you, but I truly had no idea just how unique." He raised a page from the pile he'd just placed on his desk and scanned the bottom text. "The good news is that I can find nothing physically wrong with you. You're as healthy as any twenty-something woman can be."

Jane released a breath she hadn't realized she'd been holding. "Glad to hear it. So, what is the bad news?"

Dr. Weston shook his head. "I guess the only bad news is that I have no answers for you. I don't know why you can do these amazing things. That wasn't likely something we could have answered with these tests anyway, but at least we can rule out the scary stuff."

"Scary stuff? Dr. Weston, not knowing what I am is pretty damn scary."

"I know, dear. I apologize for inferring that it wasn't. I'm just glad we didn't find anything unusual or fatal in your tests." He stood and came around the desk. Then, he leaned on the edge in front of her. "I do, however, have some friends in the science community who might be able to help."

Jane looked wary. "Can they be trusted? I don't want to be a news story, and I sure don't want to become a lab rat."

Dr. Weston tried to reassure her. "I absolutely trust them."

She sighed. "Okay then." She glanced at the paper in her hand again. "Do I really need anxiety medication?"

"Only if you want it. I know you are overwhelmed and worried. From what you've told me, that causes...incidents. If you feel out of control, I want you to have access to something that might calm you down. Obviously, this isn't an all-the-time thing. Just use it as needed."

"Thank you, Dr. Weston. I appreciate everything."

"I'm glad. Now, where is Colt? He's been by your side all week."

"He had to put in some extra hours at work today. He said something about a specialty bike coming in."

"I see." He rose and offered his arm to walk her to the door.

She stood and linked her arm in his. They made their way through the lobby.

Once they reached the front doors, he patted her hand in a fatherly gesture. "I'll contact those friends of mine, and we'll see what we can learn, okay? Until then, try not to worry about it too much."

She nodded and gave his arm a squeeze before letting go and pushing open the door.

"Jane, if you or Colt need anything at all, please don't hesitate to call me—day or night. Got it?"

"Got it." She gave him a beaming smile and exited through the glass doors.

Dr. Weston watched her leave, and then he gave his head a small shake. She was truly remarkable, and he worried that might be both a good and a bad thing.

Twenty-five minutes later, Jane arrived at Mike's Bikes.

Colt had insisted she call when she needed a ride, but it was a beautiful day, and she'd needed the walk to clear her head. She entered through the front office, and a lovely young brunette greeted her in a friendly manner.

"Hi! Welcome to Mike's Bike's! What can I help you with?"

"Hi! I'm Jane, here to see Colt Henderson, please."

The young woman's eyes went wide. "You're Jane?" She hid smirk. "I see why he can't stop talking about you."

Jane blushed, unsure of what to think about such a statement or how to even respond.

"My name is Macy. It's nice to finally meet you."

"It's very nice to meet you, too, Macy." Jane once again gave her most genuine smile, and as always, it lit up the room.

Macy started to call back to the shop when she was interrupted.

"Well, well, what do we have here?"

Jerry stood in a doorway to the left and looked Jane over in a way that made her intensely uncomfortable. He stepped closer to her, and his slightly uneven teeth formed a creepy grin while he leered at her.

"You looking for something to ride, baby?"

His meaning wasn't lost on her, despite her lack of experience.

He winked. "I'd be more than happy to help you out."

Macy rolled her eyes. "You're disgusting, Jerry. Leave her alone."

Jerry glared at Macy. "You're just jealous."

She barked out a half laugh and half snort. "You're right, Jerry. The thought of sleeping with you keeps me up at night."

He turned to her, his interest slightly piqued. "You don't say? I'd love to hear more."

Macy leaned in close and used her well-manicured index finger to motion that he should do the same.

"Yes. The thought of you in my bed…makes me wanna puke. It's my own personal nightmare."

Then, she leaned back and smiled as his face twisted from interest to fury.

"You stupid little slut. Someone's gonna shut that smart-ass mouth of yours someday." His voice was menacing.

Macy brushed it off as if he treated her that way on a regular basis.

Jane caught something about the look on his face that made her worry for Macy—or any other woman who Jerry focused his rage on. He seemed tightly coiled and ready to snap at any moment.

Just then, Colt walked through the door leading into the shop, wiping one hand on his jeans while studying a work order. He slid the paper across Macy's desk and then looked up to see Jane standing in front of him with Jerry just a few steps beside her.

"Jane? I thought you were gonna call me after your appointment."

"I was, but it was such a nice day that I decided to walk."

"You should have called me." Colt seemed agitated.

"I'm sorry. I just…" Jane realized they still had an audience.

Macy was pretending to work on the computer, and Jerry was outright mentally undressing her while giving Colt the cold shoulder.

She cleared her throat. "Can we talk someplace private?"

Colt nodded. "Sure. Let me get my keys, and I'll take you home." He ran to the shop, clocked out, and grabbed his keys.

Just as he walked back into the office, he heard Jerry's irritating voice.

"You know, Jane, Colt's pretty screwed up. If you ever wanna know what it's like to be with a real man, I'm here for ya. I'd treat you the way a woman should be treated."

Colt stepped between them. "Oh, really, Jerry? Like beating the hell out of her the way you do with Lisa?"

Jerry stuck a finger in Colt's face. "You shut your damn mouth! You don't know what you're talking about!"

Colt stepped forward until they were almost nose-to-nose. "I know exactly what I'm talking about, you cowardly sack of crap. And if you know what's good for you, you'll never lay another finger on her."

Jerry sneered and then glanced at Jane. "Yeah? Well, maybe I'll find a new hot piece of ass to touch, and you can have Lisa. I'm tired of her anyway."

That was the last straw for Colt. He grabbed Jerry by the collar and looked him in the eyes. "You so much as look Jane's way again, and I'll kill you."

"Feeling possessive, Colt? That's not like you at all. I thought you were all about getting in and getting out. She must be really good in the sack."

Colt let out a growl and pushed Jerry away, but then he lunged at the man again. Jerry let out a whoosh of breath as they fell to the floor. Colt sat up and punched Jerry in the jaw, the force of the blow slamming Jerry's head into the tiled floor. Blood oozed from his lip as he struggled to get up, and then he scrambled away.

Macy screamed for Mike, and Jane stood back, horrified. Jerry managed to get on his feet, but instead of walking away, he took a swing, hitting Colt in the left eye. Colt stumbled back for a minute and then went after Jerry again—punching him in the stomach several times. Jerry doubled over and fell to his knees. Colt was about to strike another blow when Mike walked in.

"What the hell is going on here?"

Colt spit on Jerry. "I'm teaching that piece of garbage some respect."

Jerry pulled himself up and leaned over Macy's desk. His breathing was heavy, and he appeared to be unsteady.

Mike frowned. "You two have got to cut this crap out, or I'm gonna fire the both of ya!"

Jerry let out a small laugh. "You won't have to fire Colt because I'm gonna kill him." Then, he charged at Colt with a box cutter he'd swiped from Macy's desk.

Colt blocked the first blow with his arm, but he sustained a deep gash in the process. Jerry was swinging the blade again when Jane screamed, her fear for Colt overwhelming her. The lights flickered, and every small object in the room suddenly slipped gravity's hold. Suspended in air, they hung there, as if waiting for a command.

Macy, Mike, and Colt looked on as Jerry stood completely still, frozen in fear. The box cutter was no longer in his hand. It was now floating only inches from his face. All the other objects were surrounding him, poised and ready to strike.

Jane had her eyes closed, and her hands were balled into fists in front of her face. She could see dark swirls once more, but the shapes looked familiar this time. One large shape in the middle was Jerry, and as she concentrated on him, several small dark objects levitated closer to him.

Then, her vision changed.

Jane was standing in a modest farmhouse. A man and woman were sitting on a sofa, and a redheaded girl sat between them as they snuggled together and read a storybook. She was giggling and rolling her eyes as her dad made silly sound effects to go along with words her mother was reading.

Jane stepped closer and realized she'd seen the girl before.

The girl looked up at Jane, and time seemed to stand still.

"This is where it gets scary."

Jane blinked. "What? What do you mean?"

The girl looked sad. "This is where it all starts. No one can help us now."

Jane frowned and took a step toward the girl, but she was stopped by the sound of a door being kicked in. The girl screamed as three men with guns stormed through the living room and pointed their weapons at the family. The father stood, and one of the men quickly put a gun to his head, warning him not to move.

The mother rose, placing herself between the intruders and her daughter. "I will not let you take her. She's just a child!"

The leader of the group stepped forward and looked down at the brave woman defending her daughter. "You can't stop us, so if you know what's good for you, you won't even try. Hand her over, and no one has to get hurt."

The mother glared at the man. She trembled slightly as she poked a finger at his chest. "Over my dead body."

The man laughed. "If you insist." Then, he thrust a small knife into her chest.

She let out a cry of pain and then looked down at the blood quickly staining her white blouse. Behind her, the girl screamed at the sight of her mother being attacked.

Suddenly, the entire house went dark.

Jane could only see the angry swirls once more.

Jane woke up to Colt cradling her in his arms.

He whispered near her ear, "It's okay, sweetheart. Let him go."

His voice soothed her fear, and she took in a deep breath before fully opening her eyes. Once she did, all the items came crashing to the floor in a

amy hale

clamorous mess. She looked around to find Jerry still frozen in place, sweat dotting his face. Macy and Mike gawked at her with open mouths.

Colt took her hand and led her out the door and then into his truck. Once she was buckled in, he put the key in the ignition, and the tires squealed as he pulled away.

Colt knew this was bad news. Macy couldn't keep a secret even if her life depended on it, and Mike would find a way to use this knowledge to his advantage. But Jerry would be the worst. He'd spread vicious rumors in any way he could, making Jane out to be some horrible monster and painting himself as the victim. He'd make sure everyone knew about Jane and her abilities. It would be a literal witch hunt.

Within minutes, they were pulling into his driveway.

He once again took her hand and led her inside. "Jane, pack your things. We need to go."

She blinked as if seeing him for the first time. "Go? Where am I gonna go, Colt? I have no one. No family. No home. No one!" Her voice cracked as the reality of her situation pushed through the fog in her mind.

He grabbed her upper arms and looked into her eyes. "You have me, Jane. You have me."

He pulled her to him and kissed her as if she were vital to his very existence. She stiffened for just a moment, his actions surprising her for only a few seconds. Then, she wrapped her arms around him and kissed him back. His tongue pushed past her lips, and she followed his lead. She moaned just a little, and it was enough to bring Colt back to the present.

He pushed her away to look at her face again. "I'd really like to continue this. You have no idea how much I'd like that. But we need to pack and get outta here."

She nodded and fled to the room she'd been calling home for the past week. She threw what few things she had into her small duffel bag. Her mind raced with thoughts of everything that had just happened—the fight between Colt and Jerry, the weird vision of the little girl and her parents, Colt kissing her. She didn't understand how she could be feeling so many mixed emotions at once. When they got to where they were going, she'd sort them out one at a time, but for now, she just needed to concentrate on getting somewhere safe.

Colt was in the kitchen, throwing some food into a cooler, when she came back down the hall. He'd wrapped the cut on his forearm with a bandage, but some blood was already seeping through it.

She looked at him with concern. "You might need stitches."

He snapped the cooler lid shut and glanced at her bag. "Nah, I'm okay. Ready to go?"

Jane gave him a silent nod in return. He picked up his own duffel bag and the cooler. Then, he walked out to put them in the back of the truck.

She followed and tossed her bag next to his, and then she climbed into the cab.

Once Colt had locked up, he pulled away from the house and drove toward the only place he knew would be temporarily safe. Very few people knew the exact location of the cabin, and at that moment, he was extremely grateful for that.

By that evening, word had spread about the new girl and the incident at Mike's. As things tended to happen, the truth became so stretched that it was barely recognizable once it reached the local news sources. They had gotten reports of all kinds with witnesses claiming to have seen anything from the simply odd recollection to the totally outrageous fabrications.

Local news anchor Peter Grant had a stack of papers in front of him, and he was trying to sort fact from fiction. He sighed as his intern, Emily, placed a cup of coffee on his desk.

"I can't believe this, Emily. There is no way any of this can be true, let alone all of it. It's impossible!"

She nudged his coffee toward him. "Yeah, it sounds pretty crazy."

He shuffled through the papers. "I mean, look at this! People are claiming that her hair turned into flames, and lasers shot out of her eyes. Oh...and here's a guy who is absolutely sure she's possessed by demons." He rubbed his temples. "Did someone dump hallucinogens in the drinking water?"

Emily shrugged. "Who knows? But something must have happened to start all this talk. You know how small towns are when it comes to gossip."

Peter agreed and knew he needed to get to the bottom of it. Since this girl was unknown in the area, he'd need to talk to those closest to her to learn more. He'd heard she was pretty close to Colt Henderson, which surprised the hell out of him since Colt had a reputation for avoiding relationships like the plague. Peter figured he'd start with Colt and move up from there.

But first, Peter had to figure out what to say on tonight's broadcast. There was no way he could put this story on hold when everyone in the county had likely heard about it by now. The public expected answers—or at the least, a juicy headline they could talk about until real facts were brought to light. He'd give his viewing audience a little something to wet their whistles, and then he'd give them the whole scoop once he'd done some investigating.

About an hour later, a man sat in a café just a few blocks from Mike's Bikes, sipping coffee at his booth and watching a TV placed conveniently for the patrons' enjoyment. The local news had just started, and he watched with disinterest as he picked at his dinner.

The waitress arrived and offered him a refill when something the news anchor had said caught his attention.

He held his cup out. "Can you turn that up?"

She nodded and went to the lunch counter to get the remote. She raised the volume enough, so the man could clearly hear what the broadcaster was saying, then she filled his cup with fresh coffee.

He picked up his cell phone and dialed a number. "Hey. Ben here. I think I found her."

EIGHT

BUT THEN I HURT THE ONES I LOVE,

MY SHAME AND ANGER BURN.

Peter finished up his broadcast and tiredly made his way back to his small dressing area. Confident he was ready for the prime time, he was sick of covering these small-town stories, but it was going to take an amazing feature to put his name in front of the big shots upstate. He knew the story about the Jane Doe with powers was a pretty thin thread to hang his career on, but if any of it were true, he was positive he could do the kind of investigative journalism that would boost his ratings and hopefully get him noticed on a national level.

As he'd suspected, the studio phones were ringing off the hook with people offering to share what they knew, hoping it would get them a spot or at least a mention on TV. The problem was that most of it was made up or greatly exaggerated. Everyone had a different story.

Peter had tried to contact Mike Stevens, owner of Mike's Bikes, but so far, he hadn't returned Peter's calls. Macy Lane had also been suspiciously absent from the shop and her home. Jerry Walters had agreed to speak to him later tonight, so at least that was something. Jerry didn't have a stellar reputation in the community, but he had been an eyewitness to the event and could at least provide a little more clarity.

Keys in hand, Peter left the studio with the intent of finding Colt. He and Colt were casual acquaintances, and he hoped Colt would have enough regard for him to allow him an exclusive. After double-checking Colt's address on his GPS, Peter pulled his silver Honda Civic into traffic and prayed that Colt was home. It took him less than fifteen minutes to find Colt's house, but as he pulled up front, he noticed all the lights were out.

Damn! Just my luck!

Driving away, Peter realized that he'd have to follow his only lead for now. He wasn't looking forward to spending any amount of time with Jerry, but it was all he had.

On the way to Jerry's, Peter passed The Rusty Hinge and decided to stop in just in case Colt was enjoying his favorite beverage there. Walking in, he scanned the dimly lit room and then made his way to the bar. It was unusually crowded, and the noise level was way above his preferred tolerance level.

Peter took a seat and looked around.

"Hey! You're that guy on the news, right?" James stood behind the bar, looking at Peter, while he handed a beer to a beefy man covered in tattoos.

Peter tried to smile and pretend that he wasn't completely out of his element. "Yeah, that's me. Peter Grant."

He extended his hand across the bar, and James shook it.

"I'm James. What can I get ya?"

"I'll have a beer. Thanks." Peter wasn't a huge fan of beer, but he'd drink it to keep from standing out.

James handed the drink to him, and Peter took a sip.

"Hey, James, have you seen Colt Henderson in here tonight?"

"Nah. I haven't seen Colt in several days. Since he took up with that hot redhead, he's cut back his bar time." James smiled. "Can't say I blame him. If I had that at home, I wouldn't be here either."

Peter chuckled. "She's a looker, huh? I haven't seen her yet."

James let out a low whistle and shook his head. "I'm telling ya, she walked in here one night, looking like she'd stepped off a fashion magazine. By the end of the night, she had just about every guy in the place rolling his tongue back up. Too bad the fight made them leave. I would have loved to talk with her a little more myself."

"A fight? Did some guy hit on her or something?"

James filled another beer and handed it to a waitress. "Sorta. From what I understand, that drunk slob Max pulled her into the men's room, and she kicked his ass. It was a disaster in there. She somehow managed to break every damn window and mirror we had in there. Colt came in later and gave a vague explanation. He apologized and then paid for the damages. She must know some martial arts or something. The guy's a big fella. That's him over there." He pointed to a small table near the jukebox.

Peter smiled and passed James a twenty-dollar bill and his card. "Thanks so much, James. You've been really helpful. If you hear from Colt or see him, please give me a call. I really need to talk to him."

James stuffed the money and card in the pocket of his jeans and gave Peter a nod. "Will do, man."

Peter grabbed his beer and pushed his way through the crowded dance floor until he reached Max. "Hi, I'm Peter Grant. Mind if I join you?"

Max glanced up from his almost empty glass and gave Peter a sneer. "Why the hell would I care who you are, and why would I want you to join me?"

Peter looked at Max's empty glass. "Because I'm the guy who's gonna buy your drinks for the rest of the night. All I want is a few minutes of your time and some information."

Max looked less irritated but still seemed unhappy about having company. "Sure. Have a seat."

Peter flagged down the waitress and ordered another beer for Max. "Now, I need to know what happened in the men's room when that girl Jane got into a fight with you."

Max went pale. He looked into the new beer that had just been placed before him. "I don't know what you're talking about."

"C'mon, Max. I already know most of it. I just want to hear your side of the story. I want to give you the chance to get the truth out there." Peter knew he was pulling at straws, but if his hunch was correct, this story might be bigger than he'd originally thought.

Max hesitated. "I dunno. Colt told me to keep my mouth shut, or I'd regret it. I don't wanna cross him."

"Don't worry about Colt. Something else happened with Jane today that has brought her...abilities public. I just want to make sure we've got the whole story. Nothing you could say will make things any worse for her at this point."

Max seemed to consider that for moment. "Well...if that's the case, I guess I can tell you. You're still buying the beers, right?"

"Absolutely. I'll cover it all. You just tell me what happened, and don't leave anything out."

"I had several beers and needed to take a piss, so I went to the men's room. Just as I was zipping up, this hot girl stumbled in. I thought maybe she was up for a little fun, so I started to show her a good time. I guess she changed her mind at the last minute. I had her against the wall when, out of nowhere, she tensed up, and then I was in some serious pain." He leaned forward as if afraid to speak the words too loudly. "I don't know how she did it, but every piece of glass in the room shattered, and I swear, half of it was stuck in my back and arms. I tried to protect myself, but...well, I'm gonna have some scars."

Peter had no doubt that Max deserved every scar he'd gotten. Peter tried to push past his distaste for the man, so he could get the rest of the story. "So what happened then?"

"Then, Colt bolted through the door, being all Mr. America or whatever, and he got her out of there. She was completely untouched by the glass. Colt said that I'd better not tell a soul, or he'd come after me." Max downed the remainder of his beer. "She's a witch or something. What happened in there...wasn't natural."

Peter tried not to smile as he stood up. "Thanks, Max. You've earned your drinks. I'll tell James to put the night on my tab, so have a good time. Just get a cab when you're done, got it?"

Max waved him away and then signaled the waitress for another beer. Peter passed the bar as he left and informed James of his impending bill and told him to call with the total.

Peter climbed back into his car and drove to Jerry's house. If Jerry's story was anything like Max's, Peter knew he was looking at the story of the century.

Colt was frying eggs on the small stovetop in the cabin. He was trying not to worry about Jane, but this latest display of her gifts had rattled her. She wasn't ready to talk about it yet, so he was giving her time.

They also needed to discuss that kiss, but he wasn't sure where to start. He knew he couldn't give her a long-term commitment, and the last thing he wanted to do was lead her on, but damn, he couldn't get that kiss out of his mind. He didn't know how she felt about it since she hadn't brought it up either. Maybe it didn't mean anything at all to her, and she had just reacted in the moment.

He frowned at the thought. He wanted her to obsess over their kiss at least as often as he did, and he knew that made zero sense for a guy trying to avoid commitment.

Jane stepped out of the bathroom, stretching her arms above her head. The motion made her tank top rise a bit, and Colt got a nice glimpse of her stomach. He turned back to the eggs and tried to think of anything but wanting to see more of her bare skin.

"How many eggs do you want?"

She poured herself a cup of coffee. "Just one, please. I'm not very hungry this morning."

She sat at the table and sipped her drink while staring out the window. Colt plated the eggs and toast. Then, he joined her at the table and sat her meal in front of her. He watched her for a moment and wondered if she was even aware that he was there. She seemed to be lost in her thoughts. He didn't know if he should interrupt or leave her be until she was ready to eat.

She closed her eyes and sighed. Then, she opened them and looked at Colt. "Thank you for helping me. I don't know where I'd be if it wasn't for you. What happened yesterday..." She heaved another deep sigh. "This isn't what you signed up for, Colt. Because of me, you're fighting with your coworkers, and you might have lost your job. I'm sure the rumors are flying. Your reputation could be ruined. You don't deserve that."

Colt pointed his fork at her. "Don't you worry your pretty little head about any of that. My coworkers are asshats. I couldn't care less about them. As for my job, I've been dying for a reason to quit and start my own shop, so no loss there." He took a bite of his eggs and chewed as he thought for a moment. "I've never put any stock in rumors and the small-minded people who share them. And my reputation? Anyone who really knows me won't let gossip change their opinion of me."

She gave him a shaky smile. "Oh, Colt. I don't deserve you."

He stopped mid bite and put down his fork. "You don't deserve me? Well, that's probably true. You deserve better, but sadly, you're stuck with me right now, so you'll have to make it work."

Colt gave her a small smile, but it didn't quite reach his eyes. He seemed sad. Jane didn't know who he was sad for—her or himself. She should never have involved him in her mess. She should have walked away after the incident in the bar and told him to leave her alone. It was what any decent person would have done. But she was selfish and wanted the comfort of his friendship. Even now, she felt sure she should let him go, but she couldn't bring herself to tell him good-bye just yet. He was her one source of happiness since she'd emerged from her accident with no memories.

Is it so bad that I want to be happy? With him?

She looked back down at her eggs and forced herself to eat.

Colt waited until she finished, and then he took both their plates to the kitchen. He placed them in the sink and then turned to look at her.

His odd expression made her nervous.

"What are you thinking?" she asked.

He studied her for a moment and then pushed himself away from the counter. "I'm thinking, you need a day of fun. Can you swim?"

"I'm not sure." She looked worried about the idea.

"If you get in the water and decide you can't, we'll just enjoy the shallow area. I promise, it'll be fun."

Jane eyed him with a hint of suspicion. "And just what am I supposed to wear? I don't have a bathing suit."

"No? Well, that's too bad." He gave her a wicked grin. "You do have a birthday suit though. I'm told those work just as well."

She opened her mouth, and nothing but a squeak came out, so she snapped it shut again.

Colt laughed. "I'm teasing you, beautiful. Shorts and a T-shirt work pretty well when you have nothing else."

She blushed a little, thinking about the nothing-else part. Mostly, she was wondering what it'd be like to see him in his birthday suit. That was not a path her thoughts should travel, so she stood and walked over to her duffel bag. Colt had taken her on a short shopping spree earlier in the week, and she now had a few more changes of clothes, including shorts.

She grabbed a pair of tan shorts and a yellow T-shirt. "Give me a few minutes to change."

Thirty minutes later, Jane and Colt were sitting on the bank of a large pond. Although it was early in the day, it was already getting hot, and the cool water was inviting.

Colt explained that the pond stayed pretty clear, thanks to an underground spring. He wasted no time with diving in, but Jane was hesitant. He surfaced to find her still standing at the edge of the water. She dipped one toe in and shivered, despite the heat.

"It's cold at first, but you'll quickly get used to it. It feels amazing. I promise," he said.

She nodded but still looked unconvinced.

Colt swam over to the shallow end and slowly made his way toward her. She swallowed as each inch of him came out of the water and into clear view.

He reached her and took her hand. "Would you rather just hang out here on the bank? We could just dip our feet in, if that makes you more comfortable."

She smiled at him. "No, it's okay. I just want to wade in first in case I don't swim well."

"I'll go with you." He took her hand and led her to the area where he'd just emerged.

Step by step, Jane cautiously entered the cool water. Once it reached her hips, she doubted her decision to try swimming. The water was pretty cold, but Colt hadn't lied about adjusting quickly. She let go of his hand and took a couple more steps until the water was past her waist. Then, she dunked herself under. She popped right back up and gasped at the sudden temperature change. She must have looked ridiculous because Colt was trying to suppress his laughter.

Jane slanted her eyes at him. "Oh, was that funny to you? What about this?" She cupped her hand and started splashing water directly into his face.

Colt sputtered for a moment, spitting out the water that had entered his mouth, and then he openly laughed. He gave her a taste of her own medicine. His splashes were much bigger, and she went from offense to defense in a matter of moments.

He stopped his water assault and waded out to a deeper part where he could actually swim. He showed her how to move her arms and legs as he crossed in front of her a few times. She was still nervous about trying, but he assured her that he would be right there if she needed him.

Jane tried to relax and let her arms and feet do the work, but after the first couple of strokes, she found herself sinking. She panicked, causing her body to go under for a moment. As she kicked back up to the top, she felt Colt's arms wrap around her waist. He pulled her to him with one arm and used the other to get them to a shallow spot. Her eyes closed, she clung to him as they settled near the bank.

Colt wanted to let her know that it was okay to relax, that she was safe, but his traitorous voice wouldn't work. All he could feel was her warm body pressed up against him while her arms wrapped around his neck. His reaction to her being so near was taking over any rational thought he might have had. Because she was soaking wet, he was noticing more of her than she'd probably appreciate knowing about.

Jane opened her eyes and looked up at Colt. His gaze was intense, and she felt herself struggling to breathe for an entirely different reason than the cool water that had terrified her just moments before. She swallowed the lump forming in her throat, and his attention shifted from her eyes to her lips. That did nothing to help her relax. She cleared her throat and looked at the bank just a few feet away.

While she was looking away, Colt took the opportunity to move in a bit closer. She always smelled like flowers. He wasn't sure if it was body wash or perfume, but he immensely liked it. Even after she'd been immersed in the pond, he could still catch the faint scent on her skin. He was so drawn to her in that moment that he almost nuzzled her neck. He'd gotten close enough that when she turned to face him once again, her cheek almost collided with his nose. He pulled back, loosened his grip on her waist, and then took her hand in his.

He led her out of the water and over to an area that was flat and covered in soft grass. He spread out their towels and motioned for her to have a seat. She sat down next to him and smiled as the sunshine warmed her slightly chilled skin. He leaned back and closed his eyes, so she did the same. The mutual silence was interrupted only by the occasional birdsong.

Within moments, Jane had gotten so comfortable that she fell asleep.

Colt rolled to one side and watched her. The sun played on her hair in waves of brilliant orange that almost looked like fire. Her pale skin was dotted with light freckles that seemed to make her all the more enchanting. He couldn't tear his eyes away from her.

As he watched her, he wondered how her life would play out. *He would do all he could to help her, but what then? Would she live a normal life? Would she find a husband, raise kids, and have the picket-fence life so many girls dreamed of?* He wished that he could reassure her that all would end well. He wished that he could reassure himself. When it came down to it, he didn't really know what their next move was. He just knew he needed to protect her for as long as he could. And he needed to keep his damn hands to himself.

Colt started to wonder how long he was capable of doing either.

He was still watching her when he saw her flinch. She seemed to still be asleep, so he wondered if she was dreaming. She flinched again, and he moved closer.

Jane was in the throes of a dream.

She was running, but she didn't know why. She looked back and felt nothing but fear. When she looked forward, she saw the girl who always appeared during her visions. She seemed to be running from the same thing Jane was.

"Wait, little girl! Please wait!"

The girl stopped for a moment. Then, she shook her head and kept running.

Jane tripped over a root and landed face-first onto carpet. "Carpet? Why is there carpet in the forest?"

She stood up and realized she was in a small room. Several children were playing with toys, completely unaware of Jane's presence, except for the little girl. She turned to Jane and smiled but said nothing.

Jane was puzzled. "Who are you?"

The girl looked sad. "You've forgotten me."

Jane felt guilty. Was this her little sister or a friend from her past? "I didn't mean to forget you. I was hurt. I just can't remember things."

The girl nodded and motioned to the others. "You've forgotten them, too. But they remember you, Jane. They are waiting for you."

"Why are they waiting for me? What am I supposed to do?"

The girl took Jane's hand. "Just don't be scared. You can't be scared anymore."

Jane was confused. She was about to ask what that meant when she heard a man's voice. It seemed oddly familiar.

Fear shadowed the faces of the children in the playroom, and Jane felt the fierce need to protect them. The door to the room swung open, and Jane put her hands out to protect them all.

"Jane! Jane, sweetie! Wake up!" Colt placed a hand on Jane as she writhed on the ground, trapped in her horrific nightmare.

Jane's eyes opened, and she defensively put her hands out in front of her, just as she had in the dream. "No!" she screamed.

When her hand touched Colt, he was violently thrown backward, landing in the pond with a huge splash. His shout and the jolt of power she felt rushing from her hands were enough to fully wake her. She watched, horrified, as Colt surfaced and gasped for air.

Colt splashed around for a moment to get his bearings, and then he looked at Jane. She was visibly shaking, and despite the initial shock of the moment, he needed to comfort her.

He rushed from the water and wrapped his arms around her, not caring if she might throw him backward a second time. She buried her face in his neck and tried to control her sobs. He smoothed her hair and rocked her.

"I'm so sorry, Colt! I'm so very sorry! I didn't mean to hurt you!"

"Shh...I know, Jane. It was an accident. I'm okay."

She pulled back and looked into his eyes. She worried that he'd fear her, but no matter what had happened, Colt had been supportive and affectionate. She didn't know why, but she had the distinct feeling that this level of care was something she hadn't had in a long time. She was determined to enjoy it while it lasted, but deep down, she knew it couldn't last long.

NINE

Once they came back from the pond, Jane took a warm shower and tried to relax her tense muscles.

Now, she stood before the bathroom mirror, wondering just how abnormal she really was. Physically, she appeared to be just like everyone else, but inside, something was drastically different. This particular something was dangerous and out of her control. She wondered if these so-called gifts were really a curse. Maybe her abilities had created the accident that caused her amnesia. It certainly seemed possible.

She stared at her reflection and found that she loathed her gifts. Colt might not be scared, but she was. These abilities might have separated her from her former life forever, and now, they would take away any chance she had at happiness in the future.

She knew what she needed to do. She just hoped she had the strength to do it.

She walked out of the bathroom, still towel-drying her hair, when she saw Colt sitting on the bed. He'd changed into dry clothes, and his damp hair still clung to his face and a little to his neck where it was starting to grow out. He smiled at her, and she felt her resolve weaken. When he patted the spot next to him on the mattress, she almost ran back into the bathroom, but she knew now wasn't the time to be a coward. She sat next to him, making sure there was a decent amount of space between them.

Colt looked down at his hands. "We need to talk."

Jane smiled, but it wasn't her normal optimistic smile. "I was about to say the same thing."

He turned his body toward her slightly, so he could look her in the eyes. She thought he seemed tense.

"Ladies first."

She let out a shaky breath. "I'm not sure where to start." She twisted her hands, something she'd realized was a nervous habit. "I've been having nightmares, but I don't always remember them. I'm also getting weird visions or something like visions, and they always have the same little girl in them. These so-called gifts are popping up more and more, creating damage wherever I go. I have no control over any of it. It scares me, Colt. And I worry about hurting you."

Colt reached for her hand, but she pulled back.

"You probably shouldn't touch me. It's not safe."

He frowned. "I don't believe you'd ever hurt me."

She stood up and started to pace. "Not intentionally, but this"—she made a gesture, indicating her entire body—"is unpredictable and dangerous."

He shook his head. "I don't give a rat's ass. I'm not staying away from you."

Her frustration grew. "Why not? Why can't you just walk away?" She was yelling now. "You need to let me go and never look back, Colt!"

He stood up and blocked her, so she couldn't pace anymore. "Why? You want to know why?"

She crossed her arms and nodded.

He grasped her upper arms and pulled her close. His face was just inches from hers as he looked deep into her eyes. When he spoke, his voice was soft, "Hell if I know why, Jane. But I can't walk away from you. I can't. I won't."

Jane tried not to melt against him. It took every ounce of willpower to pull out of his grasp. "What do we do then? Because I can't keep playing guessing games over what will trigger the next outburst. I could never live with myself if something happened to you."

"Nothing is going to happen to me."

She didn't say anything, and he knew that she didn't believe him.

She cleared her throat. "What did you want to talk about?" She wanted to change the subject and hoped he would drop it for now.

Colt closed his eyes for a moment. When he opened them, he walked back to the bed and sat down. "Can we sit again?"

She sat next to him but didn't say a word.

"I wanted to talk about that kiss we shared at my house."

Jane blushed a little and looked at her lap, hoping he wouldn't notice her bashfulness over the subject. He put a finger under her chin and raised her face to meet his.

"I can't stop thinking about it. And to be honest, I want to kiss you again."

Jane tried to will her heart to stop beating so loudly. Just the mention of that kiss had it pounding, and she wondered if he could hear it. She parted her lips but really had no idea what to say. Colt must have read her feelings through her expression because he smiled.

He gently placed his hands on either side of her face and leaned in close, looking into her eyes. "I'm going to kiss you again. If you don't want me to, all you have to say is no."

She knew she should say it. It was a simple two-letters, just one syllable, yet she couldn't form the word. Instead, she looked at his lips as if they were the most fascinating things she'd ever seen.

He smiled even more and closed the distance between them.

This kiss was gentle. He touched his lips to hers and held them there. Then, he pulled back ever so slightly and placed a kiss on the corner of her mouth. He continued with small kisses across her cheek until he reached her ear.

He whispered, "You're all I think about." He licked her earlobe. "You're all I want."

Jane closed her eyes and sighed. There was no way she could say no now. She wanted him as badly as he wanted her.

Colt moved one hand down to her waist while the other moved behind her neck. He carefully leaned her back on the bed and moved over her. He lowered himself just enough that their bodies touched but not so much that his weight would crush her.

Resting on his forearms, he looked into her eyes again. "You know, I'm not exactly a role model for happy relationships. I'm not really a boyfriend type. But God help me, I wish I were. If I could change for anyone, it'd be you."

She reached up to brush a lock of hair from his forehead. "Why are you telling me this?"

He caressed her cheek with the back of his hand. "Because I need you to know that I care. I just don't know if what I can offer will be enough."

She shook her head. "Just shut up and kiss me."

He kissed her again, but this time, it was with an urgency that they both felt. Suddenly, they couldn't get enough of each other. He moved from her lips to her neck, lightly sucking on the tender flesh, before making his way to her shoulder. She reached one hand up and threaded her fingers through his hair. She moaned as he ran his hand underneath her shirt, caressing her skin and causing small shivers of pleasure to run up her spine.

He moved back to her mouth and deeply kissed her once more. Then, he pulled back to look at her. Her hair was fanned out beneath her, and her lips were swollen from his kisses. He could see his desire reflected in her eyes.

"You're the most beautiful thing I've ever seen." He swallowed hard. "I can hardly believe I get to touch you."

She started to protest when he placed a finger over her lips.

"I'm not blowing smoke. I mean it." He glanced down at their touching bodies and then back to her face.

He started to say something else when she shook her head. "Did anyone ever tell you that you talk too much?"

Colt gave her a wicked smile. "Would you rather I do something else?"

For the first time since waking up in that hospital bed, Jane felt confident about one thing. She belonged to Colt, heart and soul, and she always would. That wouldn't change the future, but they had now, and that would have to be enough.

"How about you show me what you want instead of telling me about it?"

His smile disappeared. "Are you sure? This is a big step. You need to be absolutely sure."

She didn't hesitate. "I'm absolutely sure."

It took a second or two for Colt to register her answer. His grayish-blue eyes darkened with a hunger that thrilled her to her core. He took a moment to memorize the way she looked in that instant, in the midst of her desire, and then he moved in closer, his lips almost touching hers.

"I'm gonna make this, us, something you'll never forget. When you're old, sitting in a rocker on a porch somewhere, I want you to think back to today and smile. I want you to feel me, even then."

He kissed her again, and then he proceeded to show her exactly what it meant to have an experience she'd relive over and over for the rest of her life.

Jane woke up, wrapped in Colt's arms. She smiled. It was just getting dark out, and they'd spent most of the day in bed. She stretched and realized she was a little sore, but it was a good kind of sore. It was worth it. Colt was amazing, and she'd no doubt cherish this day long after he moved on.

She knew he wasn't a one-woman man. He'd said as much before she practically threw herself at him. While she'd love to have a forever with him, he never promised it, and it wasn't fair of her to expect anything more than what they had before today. She'd known that when she agreed to sleep with him. It'd seemed logical then, so she didn't understand why it hurt so much to think about now.

She shook off her somber thoughts and decided to get up and make a late dinner. When she moved, Colt's arms tightened around her and pulled her back against his bare chest.

"Where are you sneaking off to?" He kissed her shoulder and nuzzled her neck while caressing her hip.

"I thought I'd make us something to eat."

He growled and flipped her onto her back, hovering over her. "I'm only hungry for you."

He smiled in an almost predatory way, and she laughed.

"There you go, laughing at me again. You really know how to crush a man's ego."

"I'm sorry." She clamped her lips shut to stop chuckling, but it was no use. Small sounds were still escaping, and she had to close her eyes to concentrate on keeping it in.

"You will be."

Colt pressed his lips to hers, and her smile disappeared as he started working his magic on her once again. His hands were all over her, and she gasped for air as his caresses changed from soft touches to tickling. She twisted and kicked to get away, trying to talk in between laughs.

"See? This is a reason to laugh." He tickled her one more time and then smiled down at her as she regained her breath.

When she could talk again, she placed her palms on his chest. "I just learned something about myself."

"Oh, yeah? What did you learn?"

"I learned that I have a vengeful streak. You will pay for that one."

He pressed her down into the mattress, his face close to hers. "I'm looking forward to it."

He kissed her again, and after a moment, she pushed him away.

"Really though, I'm hungry. Can we get up and eat something?"

He laughed. "Sure thing, beautiful. Just promise me, we can pick up where we left off when we're done."

She was suddenly overcome with emotion, so she just smiled and nodded. His words hit hard. She'd love to pick up where they'd left off once this whole ordeal was over, but she wasn't sure it would ever be over.

Colt rolled off of her and reached for his jeans, quickly putting them on and walking to the bathroom. She rose from the bed and grabbed her shirt from the floor. Her bra had been flung over the chair, but she didn't need to put that back on since Colt had plans to disrobe her again after dinner.

She slipped her shirt over her head when she heard buzzing coming from the small dining table. She padded over and picked up Colt's cell phone. He had a text message from Dr. Weston.

Colt, not sure where you are, but if you have Jane with you, it might be best to stay out of sight for a while. Rumors are making the rounds, and it's not favorable for either of you. Jerry is saying he'll be pressing assault charges against you both. I'll keep you posted. — Doc

Jane set the phone down and closed her eyes. She was afraid this would happen. She was going to ruin Colt's life, and he was too stubborn to save himself from her.

She wiped away a stray tear and walked into the kitchen to decide on dinner. She pulled out some leftovers that Colt had packed in there just yesterday and emptied them into pans.

Colt emerged from the bathroom and watched her work. He stood behind her as she turned on the burners and set two pans on the stove. Once she finished, he pulled her back and hugged her from behind. He used two fingers to gently brush her hair aside, and he kissed the side of her neck. She leaned her head back and hugged his arms as they held her to him. "Your phone buzzed." She then pushed the text message out of her thoughts and reminded herself that she had to do this one step at a time.

She pulled away from Colt to stir the pulled chicken and green beans, so he grabbed his phone and scanned the message. He pushed the object in his pocket, then set the table and grabbed a couple of water bottles.

"Is water okay?" He held one of the bottles in the air. "I did grab a few beers, but I want you to be completely sober and consensual later."

. He wiggled his eyebrows in an exaggerated manner, and she had to stifle another laugh.

He smiled at her. "See? That's when you're supposed to laugh—when I'm being stupid."

She turned off the burners and gave him an innocent smile. "Really? Are you implying that you have times when you aren't being stupid?"

He set the water down and started walking toward her. "Oh, you will pay for that, missy!"

Jane held her hands out in front of her, defending her position near the stove. "Be very careful, Mr. Henderson. I have pans full of hot food at my immediate disposal."

Colt stopped and laughed. "I know you wouldn't do it. You're too hungry to waste the food." Then, he held his hands up. "Truce." He walked back to the table and held a chair out for her. "Shall we?"

Jane brought the pans to the table, setting them on small metal trivets, and then she took the seat he'd offered.

In town, Dr. Weston was wringing his hands and praying Colt had gotten his message. Jerry was a nasty piece of work and knew just how to start trouble. Just this morning, he'd seen Jerry sitting at Barb's Diner, talking to that news anchor. That couldn't be good news.

Dr. Weston knew there was no way Jane would have purposely hurt anyone, but the rumors were building momentum, and that would eventually catch up to her.

Making his late rounds at the hospital, Dr. Weston informed the girl behind the front desk that he was to be paged immediately if Colt or Jane called in. Her eyes widened at the mention of Jane's name, but if she disapproved, she wisely kept her thoughts to herself.

Lance was standing nearby and overheard the doctor's instructions.

"Hey, Doc! You got a minute?"

Dr. Weston glanced at his watch. "Sure, Lance. What can I do for you?"

"I heard you mention Jane. Is she okay? I've been hearing crazy rumors, and I'm really worried about her. Is she safe?"

Dr. Weston hesitated, but Lance seemed genuinely concerned for her welfare, so he brushed his doubts away. "I believe she's fine. I haven't heard from her in a couple of days, but I think she's with Colt."

Lance grimaced, and a muscle twitched in his cheek. "Colt?"

Dr. Weston frowned. "Is there a problem?"

"No. No problem, Doc. I was just hoping I could see her. I doubt Colt would allow that. He's been hovering around her like bees around honey. I can never get a moment alone to talk to her. Now that he's being her protector in all this, I won't have a freakin' chance."

Dr. Weston patted Lance on the back. "Don't worry, my boy. If it's to happen, it will. Nothing can stand in the way of what is meant to be."

Lance gave him a slightly hopeful look. "You believe in all that fate crap?"

"Indeed I do. I've seen too much to pretend that we don't all have a purpose and destiny. It might not be grand. It might just be an old man doing hospital rounds on a typical weeknight. But somehow, in the grand scheme of it all, I have my part to play. So do you, Lance. Never forget that."

Lance smiled. "Do you think we can alter our destinies?"

Dr. Weston thought about that for a moment. "I guess we can. Our decisions alter our paths, but ultimately, I think we'll still end up where we are supposed to be."

Lance laughed. "Thanks for the cryptic and confusing advice, Doc. Listen, if you find out where Jane is, please let me know. I'd really like to personally check on her."

Dr. Weston nodded and then waved before walking toward the elevators.

Lance smiled to himself. Colt might have her attention now, but fate be damned, he would find a way to make Jane notice him, no matter what it might take.

TEN

Colt watched Jane sleep. She lay on her side, facing him, as she breathed deeply. He couldn't help but think of how peaceful she looked. Her inner turmoil was temporarily banished, and he hoped her dreams would be kind to her.

She deserved something wonderful for a change. She deserved something amazing. She deserved...better than him. Yet he couldn't imagine letting her go. He'd felt sure that making love to her would be great, but it had far exceeded his expectations. Frankly, it'd surprised the hell out of him. He'd realized a little too late that she was a virgin, which made her trust in him all the more meaningful. He'd taken it slow and worshiped every inch of her.

He'd wanted to brand himself in her memory. Instead, she'd branded him.

Colt had never had an experience that even remotely touched what he'd felt with Jane in the last few hours. He had hoped that sleeping with her would help him cool his heels a bit. Once again that had backfired massively. He found that he only craved her more. He feared he would never be satisfied with a little bit of Jane.

For the first time in his life, he was considering forever. She wasn't like the women in his past. She sure wasn't like his mother. He could actually see building a life with her. Colt had never wanted that before, and it was a foreign yearning that he'd have to adjust to.

She made a cute little sighing sound and rolled over. He smiled and cuddled up behind her. Kissing her behind the ear, he draped a protective arm over her. He fell asleep, thinking of Jane and all the wonderful years he would have to spend with her.

Jane kept her eyes closed and continued to breathe deeply, faking sleep. Colt had certainly given her plenty of reasons to be physically exhausted, but she couldn't rest. Her mind was reeling with worry for him. When she closed her eyes, she would see images that she'd rather forget.

In the past, her visions had hit her almost like a trance, but since the fight with Jerry, they had been randomly sneaking in whenever she closed her eyes. She had only gotten small tidbits—a room that looked a little familiar, a child's toy, and a wooded area—but the common factor was the girl who appeared in every vision. She was always there. In the most recent visions though, she never said a word. Jane had tried to communicate, but the girl had only sadly looked at her. It was starting to creep her out.

Jane continued to lie still until she was sure Colt was lost in slumber. Then, she carefully unwrapped herself from his hold and sat up on the end of the bed. For a moment, she considered just lying back down, but she knew she couldn't. She had to do the right thing by Colt.

She quietly padded to the bathroom, gathering her clothes as she went. Once she was dressed, she pulled her hair back into a ponytail and slipped on her tennis shoes. She left the bathroom and spotted her duffel bag on a chair near the bed. She picked it up and inspected the contents. Then, she looked around for the backpack she'd seen shortly after they arrived. She knew Colt kept it on hand for hikes and it would be easier to carry than her duffel bag.

Colt shifted on the bed, and she froze, fearing he'd woken up. He shifted again and reached across the bed where she'd been sleeping. He seemed to frown in his sleep but never opened his eyes. She waited until he'd settled again, and then she continued to look for the backpack. She finally found it behind a small armchair near the fireplace. It was empty, so she quickly emptied the duffel bag of her possessions and filled the backpack with them. Then, she grabbed a couple of bottles of water from the fridge and a package of granola bars, and she stuffed them in the pack.

She picked up Colt's dark blue hoodie and held it up to her face. She inhaled and tried to memorize the slight smell of spicy cologne and the outdoors that seemed to always cling to him. She watched Colt sleep for a few minutes, and then she slipped the hoodie over her head.

She put her arms through the backpack and checked her pocket to assess how much cash she still had. Earlier in the week, Colt had given her some money for necessities, but she'd spent very little of it. Now, she was immensely glad she'd saved it.

She walked over to where he lay, bent down close to his ear, and whispered, "I'm sorry, Colt. I have to. I hope you understand someday. Please just know that I care about you, and I'll never forget our time together."

She wanted to kiss him one last time, but she was afraid of waking him up. She hesitated and then decided to risk it. Her lips softly touched his cheek. She felt the tears forming on her lashes, so she quickly stood up before they could fall on his skin. Wiping them away, she drank in the sight of him one last time, and then she quietly slipped out the front door. She needed to quickly get away because she knew the sobs threatening to choke her wouldn't stay down for long.

Colt awoke to chirping birds and bright sunshine cascading through the cabin windows. He stretched and sat up, rubbing his hands over his face. He turned with the intention of pulling Jane close but realized she wasn't in bed. He assumed she was in the bathroom, so he rolled onto his stomach and gazed at her pillow, remembering how she'd looked sleeping next to him.

Sometime in the night, he'd decided she was his future. He needed to give her time, but someday, they'd both be ready for the next step. He'd eventually buy the most amazing ring he could find—something unique to fit the woman wearing it.

He reached over to her side and frowned. The sheets were cold. She hadn't been in bed for a while. He listened for the sink, shower, or toilet, but all was silent in the bathroom as well. He got out of bed and slipped on his jeans, and then he entered the bathroom to confirm his suspicions.

He left the bathroom and headed straight for the front door, praying she was on the porch. The door was unlocked, so she had to have opened it.

Stepping outside, he looked around but saw no signs of her, and he started to panic. Running back inside, he quickly finished dressing. He slipped on his boots when he noticed her empty-looking duffel bag on the table.

Standing, he slowly walked toward it, as if he were approaching something he'd rather not see. He swallowed the lump in his throat and picked up the bag. He didn't know what she'd done with her stuff, but it sure as hell wasn't where it had been when they went to bed last night.

He turned and looked over every inch of the cabin, hoping to see some sign of what had happened to her, but nothing stood out.

Walking into the kitchen, he spotted a small slip of paper on the counter.

I'm so very sorry, but this is for the best.

Don't try to find me. Be happy, Colt. Take care.

Colt closed his eyes and gritted his teeth. He crumpled the paper in his hand and threw it on the counter.

"Son of a…"

Then, he picked up a coffee cup and chucked it at the front door with all his strength. As it shattered, he yelled, "Damn it, Jane!"

He sat down on the kitchen floor and put his head in his hands. He couldn't believe he'd let this happen. The one time he'd believed he might want to build a life with someone, she'd turned out to be just like his mother—leaving when things got too hard.

He shook his head and let out a small self-deprecating chuckle. "I'm a damn fool."

Less than two hours later, Colt had showered and packed up the cabin. After loading the truck, he locked up and climbed in the cab. A small part of him wanted to stay put just in case she came back. The larger part of him wanted to get the hell out of there and put this whole mess behind him.

He'd spent the last hour or so trying to convince himself that all he'd felt for her was lust, and he'd simply gotten caught up in the moment. She wasn't his to care for, and he really wasn't interested in that kind of responsibility anyway. Pulling out of the dirt driveway and onto the small gravel road leading to the highway, he tried to repeat those words to himself, hoping they'd stick. But he never seemed to be able to get past the thought that she wasn't his. The more it ran through his mind, the more it caused an ache deep in his chest.

Colt made it to town in less than his usual thirty minutes and drove straight to Dr. Weston's house. He parked in the alley behind the modest ranch-style home and rang the back doorbell.

Dr. Weston answered and immediately looked surprised. "Colt! What are you doing here, boy? Did you get my text message?" He opened the door wide and motioned for Colt to enter.

"Yeah, I got it."

Dr. Weston noticed Colt was unusually surly this morning. He looked out the window to where the truck was parked. "Where's Jane? Is she okay?"

Colt blew out a frustrated breath. "Hell if I know. She ran out on me sometime last night."

Dr. Weston frowned. "Did you try to find her?"

"She doesn't want me to look for her, Doc. She seems to think I'm better off without her."

"She's not, Colt. You and I both know that. She needs you, especially now that she's big news in the area."

Colt froze. "Big news? I realize what happened was freaky, but I'm sure the gossip will die down soon."

"Oh, dear." Dr. Weston paced across the small kitchen and wrung his hands. "It's not that simple anymore. A reporter has been snooping around. He claims to have an eyewitness account of more than just what happened with Jerry."

"More? Like what?"

"I don't know all of it. Something about a bathroom in a bar. Now, it's being said that she purposely started that fire at the shelter with the intent to kill people, hoping it would look like an accident."

"That's a lie!" Colt's anger was rising.

"The gossip is that she is dangerous and needs to be locked up for the safety of others. We can't let them find her!"

"Them?"

"She's being sought for questioning by the police, and the reporter has been here twice. He's convinced I'm keeping her location a secret. So, until we figure this all out, she's not safe."

Colt leaned against the wall. "Well, this morning has been full of fun surprises."

"What do we do, Colt?"

He pushed away from the wall and opened the back door. "You keep your eyes and ears open. Update me on everything happening here. I'm going to go look for her."

Dr. Weston nodded as Colt turned and jogged to his truck.

He fired up the engine, but by the time he drove the few short blocks to his own home, his truck was starting to overheat and lose antifreeze.

He pulled into his driveway and slammed his palms against the steering wheel. "Damn head gaskets!"

He switched off the engine and decided to swap the truck for his motorcycle. He backed his Harley out of his garage and rumbled toward the highway, intent on finding Jane by any means possible.

Behind him, Peter followed at a distance with the hopes that Colt would lead him right to the woman who had this sleepy little town in an uproar.

Lance had just finished his shift at the hospital and realized he hadn't eaten in hours. Grabbing a breakfast burrito from the cafeteria, he ate as he drove home. His mind was on a hot shower and his soft bed when he passed Colt heading out of town on Highway 60. Jane wasn't on the back of his Harley, and Lance assumed that meant she was alone.

He wondered if Colt had chucked her aside like every other woman he spent time with. The thought of Colt hurting Jane made him angry. He felt Jane was special, and it wasn't because of all the crazy rumors going around. He didn't believe a word of it.

Lance had felt a connection with her the first time he talked to her at the hospital, shortly after she'd started to recover from her injuries. It was only a few short minutes, but it had left him looking for excuses to see her. He'd been so busy, and those visits had been short and infrequent, but he'd enjoyed them all the same.

He thought back to the fire at the shelter. He had no doubt that whatever had started that fire was an innocent accident. When the firemen brought her to his ambulance, she had been in shock and scared. While he'd hated that Jane was not well, he had been thankful for the chance to talk to her, and he admitted to having been more than happy to treat her. After that, he had secretly been hoping that she'd want to get to know him better. Even if it meant she might have a little hero worship, as long as it had sparked her interest, he'd take it. It seemed logical to him that a patient might feel strong positive emotions toward the EMT who had treated her in her time of need. He couldn't remember an incident where that had actually happened to him, but he could certainly hope it would where Jane was concerned.

He smiled as he remembered her sitting next to him, her wet hair sticking to her face as she'd huddled under the blanket he'd given her. Once she'd recovered from the initial shock, she'd given him lots of smiles and seemed to enjoy his company—that was, until that testosterone-filled meathead Colt had shown up. Then, Jane had only had eyes for him.

It just pissed Lance off all over again that women would seem to flock to Colt without him even trying to attract their attention. He'd managed to steal pretty much every girl Lance had asked out in high school. Sure, he had to admit that Colt hadn't likely done it on purpose. They had even been friends once upon a time. But when puberty had hit, Colt had turned into an Adonis, and Lance had been left behind to be just another guy friend the girls would barely acknowledge. Add that to Colt's short flings and cocky attitude, and it hadn't taken long to drive a wedge between them.

Now, Lance was sure that Colt had tossed aside Jane, and Lance wasn't going to let this opportunity go by. He hurried home to change clothes, and then he called Dr. Weston.

"Hey, Doc. It's Lance. Do you have any idea where Jane is?"

Dr. Weston blew out a frustrated breath. "That seems to be the question of the day."

"What do you mean?"

"Everyone seems to be looking for her, and there isn't much to go on. Last time I talked to Colt, he was heading out of town to look for her."

Lance frowned. So, Colt wasn't out of the picture after all. "Where was she last seen?"

"She was at Colt's cabin. He has a little spot of land not too far from the Ohio River. But she snuck out sometime during the night."

Lance remembered that cabin. Mr. Henderson had taken Colt, Brett, and Lance there for a weekend when they were boys. He didn't remember exactly where it was, but he had a rough idea.

"Thanks, Doc. I'm gonna look for her, too. If you hear anything, please let me know."

"Glad to, son. I hope you fellas find her. She needs us right now."

"I'll find her. I promise."

Lance hung up the phone and grabbed his keys. His first concern was finding Jane and keeping her safe. If he found her before Colt, well, that would be a huge bonus in his favor. He wasn't sure what Colt's plan was, but he was going to follow the highway. She had to eat and sleep somewhere, so hopefully, someone had seen her.

Jumping in the driver's seat, he wasted no time in following the same route Colt had started on earlier that morning. He needed to find her. Colt could have anyone he wanted, but Lance only wanted Jane. This might be his only chance to prove himself to her.

Colt pulled off the highway and onto a dirt road not far from his cabin. He knew of some trails that Jane could have followed, so he thought it'd be best to check those first. He hated himself for not doing this sooner. He should have taken the trails right after he'd realized she was gone, but he had just been so damn angry that he wasn't thinking straight. He parked the bike behind a utility shed that had been there for as long as he could remember. It didn't appear to be used anymore, but it'd work for keeping his motorcycle out of sight while he searched.

He jogged down the narrower of the two trails, knowing Jane would likely take the less popular path to avoid interacting with anyone. As he walked, he looked for any signs that she'd been there, anything that would tell him he was on the right track. She probably wouldn't purposely litter, but maybe she had accidentally dropped something or snagged her clothes on a limb. He had several hours before sunset, so he could cover some decent ground between now and then.

He'd been walking for about an hour when the sun glinted off an object and caught his attention. It was the shiny silver interior of a small piece of wrapper. Upon inspection, he realized it was from a granola bar. In fact, it was the same kind he kept at the cabin. He felt sure this was evidence that he was going in the right direction.

He continued to walk, hoping to find more, but after another couple of hours, he was back near the beginning where the shorter trail circled around and met with the larger one. If she had gone this way, she would have eventually left the path. He worried about her being lost in the woods. It could be a dangerous place once the sun went down. He needed a different strategy if he was going to locate her soon.

ELEVEN

MY STEPS ARE HEAVY, AS IS MY HEART,

THE PAIN, IT CALLS FOR DEATH.

Jane walked along the tree line, doing her best to stay out of sight. She kept the highway in view, so she wouldn't get lost, but she didn't want to be seen either just in case Colt or, worse yet, the police were looking for her. She had no idea what Jerry had told everyone or even what she was lawfully obliged to do in this case, but she knew getting arrested wasn't going to help her situation.

She'd been walking all day, and she was getting tired. The clouds were starting to roll in, and she feared she'd end up soaked before the day was up. Since she had nowhere to stay for the night, she thought it'd be best to look for some kind of shelter. Maybe she'd get lucky and find a hunting blind or abandoned shed where she could spend the night. It wouldn't be near as comfortable as Colt's cabin, but anything would be better than sleeping in the open.

The thought of Colt knotted her stomach. By now, he would have seen her note, and he was probably angry with her. She half-expected he'd chase her down, but so far, he hadn't caught up to her. She should be happy about that, but if she were honest, she was hoping that maybe she meant enough to him that he wouldn't let her go. She realized how selfish that was. She'd left to keep him safe, so hoping he would find her would defeat the purpose of running in the first place.

She stopped and placed her palm against the bark of a tree. Then, she placed her forehead on the back of that hand and leaned into it. She closed her eyes and groaned. She didn't really know what she wanted anymore. She was lonely and afraid. The part of her heart that hadn't stayed behind with Colt was breaking. With each step that had carried her away, her hope had died a little more. She felt sure that she would be nothing but an empty shell before she found her answers. But she thought that might be a good thing. Numb would surely be preferable to the agony she was experiencing.

In reality, she didn't know where she was even going. She needed a better plan than getting away from Colt. Maybe she should call Dr. Weston about those friends of his, if he was still willing to help.

She sighed and pushed back from the tree, wiping the tears she hadn't realized she'd shed. A low branch was just in front of her, and she reached out to touch one of the new green leaves attached to it. She rubbed her fingers over the rough surface as she contemplated her situation. She had no idea how to fix any of the problems she faced. Another tear rolled down her cheek, and she let it fall freely. She closed her eyes as a few more followed.

When she opened her eyes, she noticed the leaf in her hand had wilted to nothing but a brown dry replica of its former self. She gasped in horror as she dropped her hand, and she watched the now dead leaf break off from its perch and fall to the ground.

Her hands shook. *Did I cause that?* Her mind reeled at the thought.

She took a few steps backward, and then she turned and ran. She was heading in the opposite direction of the highway she had been so carefully following, but she no longer cared. Her very existence was a menace to all living things around her. She truly felt that she would be better off dead than living a life full of destruction. She was a disease that needed to be disposed of before her poisoned existence could infect anyone else.

As she ran, she stumbled and landed just outside the line of trees. She was tempted to curl into a ball and stay there until the elements or wildlife relieved the planet of her miserable presence. Yet some small part of her was still beating inside, pushing her to keep trying. It was a force that suddenly had more control over her actions than anything she'd experienced so far.

Picking herself up, she brushed off the dirt and took in her surroundings. Before her was a vast field of wildflowers. The sheer beauty robbed her of her voice. She slowly walked toward the middle, looking at the different varieties of colors and sizes. She stopped and sat down, inspecting a tiny purple bloom. She had no idea what it was called, but it was her favorite. These little flowers seemed to dominate the area, giving the field an overall hue of lavender. She would never have guessed that such a treasure existed inside the confines of the frightening wooded exterior.

Curious, she picked up one bloom and gently held it in her palm. Then, she closed her eyes and thought about her sadness. When she peeked through her lashes, the flower was shriveled and black. She frowned, and then she picked another bloom and again placed it in her open palm. When she closed her eyes, she thought about Colt and the wonderful day they had spent together. She saw a multitude of bright colors behind her eyelids, which seemed to happen when she was happy. This time, when she peeked, the flower was unharmed.

Jane smiled a little. "Hmm...I wonder."

She spent a few minutes pulling up a handful of grass, weeds, and flowers rooted before her. Then, she smoothed out the dirt and placed her palms down, feeling the cool soil beneath her hands. She again focused on things that brought her joy. As she did so, she felt a slight tickle under her fingers, and she opened her eyes.

Pulling her hand back, she continued to look at the patch of dirt as she embraced the slivers of joy she was feeling. She sat there, amazed, as the soil moved aside, and lovely green shoots rose from the depths of the ground. They continued to rise and then bloom, filling the area she'd touched with more beautiful flowers.

Her troubles temporarily forgotten, she cleared another small spot, again placing her hands on the dirt. This time, she closed her eyes until the colors became a purple flower, like the first one she'd touched. She willed them to grow. She opened her eyes and watched the bare area come alive with nothing but little purple blooms.

This could be her answer. She wouldn't have to hide if she could learn to control her abilities, and out here in the wilderness, away from everyone, seemed like the perfect place to practice.

The sky above her rumbled as a reminder that rain was coming, but she didn't care.

Let it come. She'd find a way to deal with it because she now knew that she was capable of more than destruction.

The first cool drop hit her on the top of the head, and she looked up. Another hit her cheek and then her forehead. She simply grinned and looked at the cloud above her. It began to rain a little harder, and she continued to look at the cloud as best as she could, despite the rain.

Without conscious thought, she instinctively lifted a hand to the sky and imagined that the cloud above her was white, fluffy, and free of rain. She brought her hand back to her side, and in an instant, the rain over her had stopped. Sun shone through the cloud, filtering it directly above and around her. The other clouds were still dumping their contents all around, but her little spot was sunny and dry.

She looked at her hands. "Oh my Lord, I knew how to do that. How did I know that?"

She continued to stare at her hands in awe. Her past had to have something to do with this. Maybe she'd already known how to control this, but she simply couldn't remember now. It'd appeared that she was acting on intuition at times even though her previous episodes were when bad things were happening.

Was it self-preservation? Were my powers protecting me subconsciously?

These were more questions that needed answers.

She stood and dusted off her hands. Knowing she'd get wet, she went back to the tree line, but before she left, she looked to the sky. Her hands at her sides, she slightly lifted her palms upward and closed her eyes. The wind began to pick up and slowly swirl around her. Her long red tresses waved and swayed with the current. She exhaled a steady breath and made each hand into a fist. The wind died down, and the entire sky was calm for just a moment. When she released her clenched hands, the cloud above her released its contents in a small torrent, and the rest of the sky quickly joined in.

As she stood in the midst of wind and rain, Jane smiled. Each brush of the wind and every drop of rain on her skin felt like a new beginning.

Colt made it home just as the rain had reached town. He'd managed to outrun the weather but not his tail. That nosy reporter had followed him home. He didn't know how long Peter had been there, but Colt knew the reporter was hoping that he would find Jane. The good news was that if he was following Colt, Peter still had no idea where she was either. She was at least safe from the attention-seeking moron for now.

Colt climbed off his bike and walked to the edge of the open garage door. Then, he crossed his arms and stared at the dark-haired reporter parked across the street.

Please do something stupid, so I have a reason to beat you senseless.

He started imagining the many ways he could get today's workout in, and it all involved his fist repeatedly hitting the news anchor.

Peter was looking at something on his phone, but when he looked up, he realized Colt had spotted him. They made brief eye contact, and then Colt dropped his arms and stalked toward Peter's car. His expression was menacing, and Peter had no trouble seeing Colt's tattoos jumping as his biceps flexed. Peter quickly decided that this was not the time to ask Colt for a chat. He started his car and sped off before Colt had finished crossing the street.

Clenching his fists and itching to vent his frustrations on someone, Colt watched the coward drive away. He then returned to his house and tried to concentrate on another plan to find Jane. As he unlocked the door, he heard the familiar strains of metal coming from the living room. He tossed his keys on the kitchen counter and grabbed a beer from the fridge. He entered the living room to find Brett peeling the label off of his bottle. His brooding expression was all Colt needed to see to figure out what had happened.

Brett glanced up from his bottle and then resumed his peeling. "Hey, Colt."

"Hey." Colt took a seat next to him. "So…who was she?"

Brett sighed. "No one important…anymore." He took a sip of his beer.

Colt heaved a sigh of his own. "Yeah. I think I know the feeling."

Brett raised his eyebrows. "You? Ha! Colt Henderson never feels anything."

Colt chuckled. "I have feelings, dumbass. I'm just careful about who I share them with."

"I guess I should have taken a cue from you for a change." Brett frowned and set down his bottle.

"No, I'm the last person you should mimic." Colt looked at his hands and thought about the last time he'd touched Jane. He needed to touch her one more time. He needed to know that she was okay.

"Colt? You look worried. What happened?"

"You mean, you haven't heard?"

Brett rolled his eyes. "I'm not a hermit. Of course I've heard, but rumors have never bothered you before." He then realized Jane wasn't with Colt. "Where is she anyway?"

"I wish I knew. That's why I'm worried. She bailed because she's scared, and now, I can't find her."

Thunder cracked, and both men looked out the large bay window to see the rain falling in sheets as the dark of night settled in around them.

"Is she outside? In this?"

Colt rubbed a hand over his face in frustration. "Damn, I hope not. But she ran from the cabin, so there's no telling where she went."

Brett studied his brother. He'd never seen Colt so upset over a woman. To anyone else, Colt would look cool and collected. But Brett knew him better. His jaw was doing that little twitch that signaled he was unhappy, and he couldn't seem to sit still. Brett knew that meant he was impatient. He wanted to find Jane, and he wanted to find her now.

"Hey, man. I don't have anything going on for the night. I'll help you look for her."

Colt glanced out the window again as the wind picked up and lightning flashed in a violent display. "We probably shouldn't be out in this. It's looking dangerous out there. I can't help but worry about her though."

Brett gave his big brother a reassuring pat on the back. "We'll let the scary stuff die down. We can't help her if we get ourselves hurt." Just then, a wind gust picked up and sent some of the lighter things in the yard rolling. "Or get killed by a tornado. That certainly wouldn't be good for any of us."

It was Colt's turn to reassure Brett. He'd been terrified of tornados since he was little boy. Anytime the wind got really bad, he'd seek Colt for assurance and comfort.

"We can't go out in this. We'll wait until it passes and then look for her. She's a smart lady. She'll be somewhere safe."

Colt wasn't sure who needed convincing more, but he wasn't wrong about Jane being smart and resourceful. She'd be fine until he could get to her. She had to be.

TWELVE

Jane was exhausted.

She'd been practicing with her gifts all night. Some things were naturally coming to her, but others were taking more work. She'd learned her emotions played a large part—not only in what she controlled, but also how intense the event would become. At times, she'd felt the power surging through her in such acute strengths that she feared it would completely consume her. She knew her lack of sleep and proper meals weren't helping, but she wasn't comfortable with returning to civilization—particularly Colt—until she was sure she would never lose control again.

She sat on a fallen tree and pushed herself to try one more time. Her hands were shaking as she closed her eyes and visualized her fears. As always, the first thing she saw was Colt's body sailing through the air, but in this instance, he didn't land safely in the water. Instead, he landed on the bank, lying there in a broken heap. It made her stomach turn, but she knew she had to face her fears of hurting him, or anyone else, and then turn them to her advantage. She'd tried envisioning others, like Dr. Weston or Carol, but Colt always incited the strongest response, so it was natural to focus on that image.

The weather had cleared hours ago, but as she worked through her emotions, she felt the wind stirring back to life and heard the distant claps of thunder. Fully immersed in her sorrow, she opened her eyes. Unlike her previous attempts, she could actually feel her anguish, as if it were a physical object. She glanced down at her hands. With one palm open to the sky, she wrapped her fingers around a dark mass that continually changed form.

Bringing the object closer to her face, she studied it. It called to her, trying to draw her back into its depths, but this time, she refused to bow. She raised her other hand above it and took a deep breath. When she exhaled, she forcefully brought her palms together, attempting to crush the mass into oblivion. The moment she extinguished the fear, a blast emanated from her hands, shooting around her so savagely that it cleared several surrounding trees of their leaves and broke their limbs.

She sighed in relief. She'd finally done it. She'd controlled and crushed her anxiety. It hadn't been perfect, but if she continued to work on it, she knew she could eventually master these gifts.

She smiled and blew out a shaky but exhilarated breath. That was when she first noticed something wasn't right. Her hands were raw and looked slightly burned. Then, she felt something running down her neck. Reaching up to touch just under her ear, she felt a sticky wet substance. Pulling back her hand, she discovered blood.

Jane frowned. She became light-headed and found herself clinging to the bark she was sitting on. The forest was starting to spin. She stood and grabbed another nearby limb to keep her balance. Using the trees to keep herself upright, she attempted to move herself toward the rising sun. She'd stashed her backpack in a log near a walking path, and she needed to get to it.

As she stumbled closer to the path, the sun seemed to change directions. She shielded her eyes with her fingers, trying to see past the blinding light source. "What? How is that possible?"

The intense light dimmed, and she dropped her hand but saw nothing. She could still see the sun in its natural position in the sky. Confused, she stepped forward once more, only to be blinded again by another ball of light. She tightly closed her eyes, begging the sudden pounding in her head to stop.

Then, she heard voices.

"Am I dead?" she thought aloud.

"What? Hey, are you okay, lady?" Two young men were standing in front of her on the path.

She nodded. "I don't know." She raised a hand to her head.

"Oh, man, she's bleeding! Marty, get that bandana out of my pack."

Marty quickly obeyed his friend. The next thing Jane knew, a cold and wet cloth was being pressed to the side of her head.

"What's your name? I'm Jake, and this is my friend Marty."

Jane looked at Jake. "I'm…I'm Jane." Then, she saw the bright light once more, quickly followed by complete blackness.

Jane woke up in a hospital bed. An IV was sticking out of one arm, and she had a pulse meter on one of her fingers. She blinked, looked around, and groaned.

Not again!

She was thankful that at least she didn't have amnesia this time—or rather, any more than she'd had when she came in. She did have to admit that she had no idea how she'd gotten there. Her last memory was of not feeling well and trying to get to her backpack and then running into two guys walking along the trail.

She frowned as she started to remember the odd lights that had faded in and out. If the guys who had helped her saw them, she hadn't caught a visible reaction from them.

She leaned her head back and looked at the ceiling tiles. Her head still hurt a bit, so she reached up to rub her temples. She was again besieged by the bright light, and her headache intensified.

"Ah!"

A nurse came pushing through the curtains surrounding her, concern on her face. "Are you okay, sweetie? Are you in pain?"

Jane nodded, still rubbing her head.

"I'll go get the doctor and see what we can give you." She hurried out of the little enclosure.

Jane could hear voices, lots of them, all talking at once. She shook her head, trying to dislodge them somehow, but they continued. She heard a man talking about his injured leg. Another woman was asking if she had appendicitis. A small child was crying, and his mother was assuring him that the shot he was going to get would be over quickly.

I'm in an emergency room. I can hear them all as if they were talking directly to me.

The pain in her temples soared again, and she closed her eyes. Then, she heard a different voice, and all the other sounds faded into the background.

"Alice? Alice, honey, you need to wake up. You need to go. Now."
A man's face loomed in front of her, slightly out of focus. "I said, go. Now. You can't stay here."

Her eyes flew open, and she felt the overpowering urge to leave. She reached down and took the pulse monitor off and then pulled the IV out, not caring about the blood that started to run down the back of her hand. She carefully stood, testing her legs. She was thankful that she seemed to be capable of walking and that she was still dressed in her own clothing.

She peeked through the curtains, watching two nurses strolling by on their way to an enclosure near the end of the area she was in. She glanced around, taking note that it must be a large hospital. It certainly wasn't the emergency room Colt had taken her to. There were dozens of bays, just like the one she was in, and staff seemed to be everywhere.

She didn't care if they saw her. She was going to leave, and they wouldn't stop her. They couldn't. Determined, she pushed through the curtains and turned to her right, seeing the Exit sign above a set of double doors. She was only a few feet away when she heard a woman behind her.

"Miss! Miss! You can't leave yet. The doctor hasn't looked at you yet! You have forms to fill out!"

Jane just kept walking.

"Miss! I must insist you stop!"

Jane pushed through the double doors. Without looking back, she made a small flicking motion with her wrist, and the doors quickly closed behind her. She left the building and was crossing the parking lot when she heard a familiar voice calling her name.

"Jane! Is that you?"

She turned to see Lance jogging toward her. His smile was wide as he approached her.

She smiled back brightly. "It's good to see you, Lance!"

"It's great to see you! Are you okay?"

She nodded. "Sure. Why wouldn't I be?"

He glanced back at the doors to the emergency room. "Well, to be honest, I've been looking for you. A friend works here, and he called me, saying a woman fitting your description had been brought in earlier. I was worried, so I rushed down here."

She stepped closer and gave Lance a hug. "Thank you for caring. That's very sweet of you."

He gave her a lingering hug back and shrugged in a slightly embarrassed manner.

"Why were you looking for me?"

Lance wanted to tell her, but the last person he wanted to talk about was Colt, so he only told her part of the truth. "I was hoping we could talk. I've been wanting to for weeks, but it never seemed to work out."

Jane didn't know what they had to talk about, but it was nice to see a friend right now. "Sure. I'm guessing you have a vehicle here. Could we go somewhere else?" She nodded behind her. "I just kinda escaped, and I don't think they are too happy with me."

Lance looked back at the doors just as two frustrated hospital employees emerged and then pointed at her. He grabbed her hand. "C'mon!"

They ran, hand in hand, across the parking lot until they reached his car. He opened the door for her, and she hopped in. Then, he rounded the front of the car and jumped in the driver's seat. He quickly pulled out of the parking lot, and Jane started laughing. Lance gave her a sideways glance as she held her stomach and tried to suppress her amusement.

She wiped a tear from her eye. "I don't know why that was such a big deal. You'd think I just escaped from Alcatraz or something. But, honestly, running felt good. It felt right."

Lance didn't know what to make of that.

She glanced at him. "I know. I'm not making sense. I promise, I'm fine. I just have some jumbled thoughts…and maybe…"

He urged her on. "Maybe?"

"Well, I wonder if I'm starting to remember some things. Maybe just a little."

Lance nodded. "That's good, right?"

She stopped to think about that. *Was it good?* She wasn't sure. She hoped so, but somehow, she suddenly couldn't get very excited about the prospect. A few days ago, she would have begged for any information on her identity. Today, she wasn't sure if it mattered anymore.

She changed the subject. "Can we go somewhere to eat? I'm starving. I don't have much money on me, but I should have enough for a meal."

He nodded. "Absolutely. And keep your money. Lunch is on me."

He steered his car toward the highway and drove downtown, the opposite direction of the little town he'd called home all his life. He knew going back home would run the risk of running into Colt.

Lance was thankful he'd found her, and he was going to take advantage of having her all to himself for as long as possible. He needed to make her forget about Colt, and that would take time. Today, he'd lay the foundation.

Jane was enjoying a large plate of fried chicken and mashed potatoes. She felt like she hadn't eaten in weeks. Lance was picking at a chef salad and watching her with amusement. She had been raving about how amazing the food was since her first bite.

She glanced at the glass case near the counter, loaded with a variety of pies. "I wonder if their pie is just as good."

Lance smiled. "I guess we'll have to find out." He called a waitress over. "One slice of…" Then, he looked to Jane for a flavor.

"Cherry. Cherry pie, please."

Lance nodded. "Cherry it is."

The waitress left to cut a slice of pie as Jane finished up the last of her potatoes and gravy. The pie arrived with a nice dollop of whipped cream on top.

The waitress looked at Jane and grinned. "You're such a cute little thing. I have no idea where you're putting all that food, honey, but I sure wish I had your metabolism. All I have to do is look at a carb, and I gain ten pounds." She handed Jane and Lance a fork and then removed his mostly empty salad bowl. "Enjoy, you two!"

Lance looked at the fork and smiled. "Sorry. She must think—" He stopped himself. He'd wanted to use the word *couple*, but he was afraid if he'd said it, she'd deny it was possible. He didn't want to hear that or give her a chance to feel uncomfortable with the idea.

She expectantly looked at him. "Think what?"

"Uh…she must think we are sharing."

"Why not? You were gracious enough to buy, and I'm not opposed to sharing dessert with you." She winked and pushed the plate to the middle of the table where they could both reach it.

Lance smiled and gestured for her to take the first bite. "After you."

She dug in and brought a large forkful to her mouth. Lance did the same. He looked up to see her licking the whipped cream off her lips, and they both started laughing.

Then, she stopped abruptly and looked nervous.

"What, Jane? What is it?"

She continued to stare, and he realized she was looking over his shoulder. He glanced up to see Colt standing there. His eyes were trained on Jane. He seemed calm, but Lance could sense the underlying tension between them. Colt had yet to acknowledge his presence, but Lance felt sure that was by design. Anyone could see that Colt wasn't happy that Jane was here with Lance.

A small part of Lance reveled in knowing that, for once, Colt was on the receiving end of jealousy. Another part of him worried that Colt really was jealous, meaning he did indeed actually care about Jane. If that were true, he wouldn't let Lance take her away from him without a fight.

Jane summoned the courage to speak first, "Hi, Colt."

He continued to look at her, his features hard. "I was worried about you."

She sighed. "I'm sorry. That wasn't my intent."

He turned his head just enough to look at Lance from the corner of his eye, and then he moved his attention back to her. "I think I see your intent pretty clearly."

Lance became irritated, "Now, wait just a minute, Colt!"

Colt leaned down and put his face directly in front of Lance's. "No, you wait a minute. Unless she's filled you in on the intimate details of our relationship"—he gave her a pointed look with the question clear in his eyes, and she shook her head, so he turned back to Lance—"which she just confirmed she hasn't, you don't know what you're walking into. I suggest you take a step back."

Lance narrowed his eyes at Colt. "Those details don't matter to me. Jane is all I care about."

Colt stood up and crossed his arms, looking between the two of them. "You don't even know her. How can you care about her?"

"I know her well enough to know that she deserves better than you!" Lance was getting more furious with every moment.

Colt glared at Lance. "You think you're the better man? Prove it! Outside!"

Lance stood and threw enough money on the table to cover the bill and tip, and then he followed Colt outside. Jane groaned and rushed out behind them.

Both men were staring each other down, and they were just moments from one of them taking a swing. Without thinking, she stepped between them.

"Jane, get out of the way," Colt growled.

"No, Colt! I'm not moving."

Lance spoke this time, "Jane, please move. I don't want you to get hurt."

She looked at Lance. "I don't want you to get hurt either! I like you, Lance, and I would never forgive myself if Colt hurt you because of me!"

Lance wasn't a scrawny guy, but he was no match for someone the size of Colt. He knew that, but he wasn't about to back down. He felt he was fighting for Jane's honor. But after she'd practically said he wouldn't stand a chance in hell, his fortitude faded a smidge.

Colt, on the other hand, was barely keeping his temper in check. "You like him? What do you mean, you like him?"

His jealousy was overriding his ability to think. Hearing her admit she liked Lance made him see red. She wasn't supposed to like him. She wasn't supposed to be here with him, sharing pie and laughing. None of this was how it was supposed to happen. She belonged with Colt.

Colt moved to step around her, only thinking that she couldn't spend time with a dead man. Lance reacted by standing a little taller and preparing for whatever Colt was ready to dish out. Jane wedged herself between them once more, and this time, she put a hand on each of their chests. She let her frustration seep through her fingertips, just enough that both men couldn't move. They stood there, almost frozen in place by her touch. They both looked at her, puzzled.

"Now, you are both going to shut up and listen to me for a change. Got it?"

They both nodded.

"Lance, you're a nice guy. I'm glad we're friends. And I really appreciate the meal and the ride today. I hope we will always be friends."

She watched some of the light dim in Lance's eyes. She felt bad for him, but she couldn't allow him to think they were anything more than friends.

"And, you!" She turned her head to address Colt. "You have no right to be angry! You made it very clear that what we had was temporary. If you're mad because I'm the one who walked away, you need to get over yourself."

Colt opened his mouth, and she dug her fingers into his chest causing him to close it again.

"I want to make this clear, Colt. You don't own me."

She glanced between the two of them. "No one owns me. I'm not a toy to be fought over. Do you understand me?"

They both nodded once again.

"Good!"

She removed her hands, and both men took a deep breath and rubbed their chests. Lance looked slightly horrified by her touch where Colt was trying to hide a grin as he watched her.

She turned to Lance and leaned forward, kissing him on the cheek. He tried hard not to flinch, but she noticed the almost imperceptible movement. It made her sad to think Lance was bothered by her gifts even if only a little.

"Thank you again, Lance. I'll hopefully see you soon. Right now, Colt and I need to talk."

Thirteen

Lance said his good-byes and drove away with the promise that he would be available anytime Jane needed a friend. Colt had done his best to stay out of their final conversation even though he still didn't like the way Lance looked at her or talked to her—or that he thought about her at all.

Damn, I am jealous.

This was another new experience for him. He normally didn't give a crap about what his lady friends did or whom they did it with. With Jane, he felt as if he could easily dismember any man who even glanced at her. He had the profound sense that Jane had changed everything he ever believed about relationships, and she hadn't even tried.

Over the years, many women had attempted to change Colt's view of commitment. He'd wanted casual flings, and they'd wanted a future filled with a house, kids, and toys in the yard. He'd never wanted any of that— ever.

Then, some wisp of a girl had fainted on his porch, and his life had changed forever. He couldn't figure out how it had happened. He still wasn't sure he wanted the whole family-life thing, but he did know the last couple of days of looking for Jane had been total hell. She'd left him feeling empty, and he never wanted to feel that again.

Jane stared at Colt. He gave her a smile that would have had most women ready to disrobe, but Jane only frowned at him.

"We need to talk." She continued to frown at him.

"Yeah, you said that." He gave her an amused smirk.

She sighed. "Colt, I'm serious."

"So am I. I've never been more serious in my life."

"Why are you smiling at me like that?"

"Because I'm so damn happy to see you." The playfulness faded, and his smile transformed into something a little more serious. "I was really worried about you."

She took a moment to study his face. He looked tired.

"I'm sorry, Colt. I didn't mean to scare you. I just needed some time."

He tried to hold his temper in check. "Time? Away from me? So, you could run off and spend time with Lance?"

She smacked his arm. "No, you idiot. I needed time alone. I just happened to run into Lance when I was leaving the hospital."

"Hospital? Why were you in a hospital?"

"It's a long story. How did you find me anyway?"

He sighed. "I was making a run up the highway, hoping to find you. That's when I noticed Lance's car here and thought I should check with him."

She nodded. "Can we go somewhere else to talk? I don't really want to do this in the parking lot."

Colt nodded as he pulled his keys from his pocket, and he turned to walk toward his motorcycle.

She followed behind him, looking for his truck. "What happened to the pickup?"

"It's not running, so I'm using the bike."

As they got closer, she hesitated. She was trying to be strong. Just the sight of him made her spine tingle, and then he had given her that smile, and she'd been struggling to keep her knees from collapsing. Being on the back of his bike with her arms wrapped around him was not going to help her resolve one bit.

He climbed on and then watched her cautious approach. She looked nervous.

"C'mon, Jane. I don't bite—unless you want me to." He gave her an exaggerated eyebrow wiggle that had her fighting back a grin. He patted the seat behind him. "Hop on. I didn't bring my helmet. Do you mind not having one?"

A helmet was the least of her worries. "No, I don't mind."

She reached up and put a hand on his shoulder to steady herself. She placed one foot on the peg and then swung the other leg over the seat. She adjusted herself into a comfortable position and then put her hands on his waist.

She leaned forward. "Where are we going?"

"I thought maybe back to the cabin."

She didn't want to go back there, not yet. There were too many memories that might sway any ability to think logically, assuming she still could. "Can we go somewhere else?"

Colt gave her an odd glance but didn't comment on her reluctance to visit the cabin. "Sure. We can't go back to my house yet, so I have another idea."

He started the bike, and she gripped him a little tighter. He smiled and enjoyed the feel of her pressed against his back. He pulled out of the parking lot and made a left turn. He drove for less than a mile before he made another left. This was one of his favorite riding routes. He loved the beauty of the countryside, the lonely back roads, and the various curves that gave him a feeling of freedom. He drove for several miles, taking her past all his prized spots.

Jane tightly held on to Colt and watched as fields, trees, and creeks passed by. It was almost serene. She knew she probably shouldn't, but she couldn't help but smile and enjoy being so close to Colt. The wind was blowing her long hair out behind her. It felt amazing even if it would take a miracle to get the tangles out later. She felt like she was flying.

If only that were one of my gifts, too…

She chastised herself for the thought.

Then, I really would be a freak.

Colt glanced at her through his side mirror. She had her eyes closed, a smile graced her beautiful face, and her hair looked like a trail of fire behind her. She was mesmerizing. He wanted to always make her smile. He had to be sure she never shut him out again. Determination took root in his mind. He'd do whatever it took to make her see that they needed each other.

He continued to drive until he came to a small town of less than four thousand people. He knew of a little place on the outskirts where they could have some privacy. He pulled the bike into a circle drive that sat in front of a modest brick house, and then he turned off the engine.

Jane relaxed her grip and then carefully slipped off the seat until her feet were on the concrete driveway. Colt dismounted the bike and stuck the key in his pocket. He reached for Jane's hand, but she quickly stuck them both in the pockets of her hoodie—or rather, his hoodie. He hid a smirk and walked to the front door. He pulled back a loose brick near the door, retrieved a key, and replaced the brick.

Jane stared. "How did you know that was there?"

Colt shrugged. "This house belongs to a friend. He's a trucker, so he's rarely here. He has me check on things for him every now and then."

He unlocked the door and pushed it open, and then he gestured for her to enter first. She crossed the threshold and looked around at the neatly furnished little house. It lacked clutter but also lacked that personal touch that indicated someone had made this house a home. She heard Colt enter behind her before shutting the door.

Then, she heard the lock click. She turned to see Colt staring at her like he was dying of thirst, and she was the only water for miles. She cleared her throat and tried to look at anything but him.

He took a couple of steps in her direction, and she took a couple of steps backward. He smiled then and continued to get closer. She backed up until she could go no farther without turning. Her lower body was against the back of a loveseat. He sauntered forward until he was directly in front of her. She had no choice but to look at his face. His smile was still in place, and his eyes roamed her face and body like a caress.

She needed to break the silent tension. "Colt, listen—"

He put a finger to her lips. "No. I have something I need to say first."

Jane nodded, and he lightly moved his finger to stroke her bottom lip. Then, his hand moved to her face, and he cupped her jaw. Her breath hitched at the familiar touch. She'd missed it badly the last couple of days, but she wasn't about to admit that to him.

He seemed to know what she was thinking. He leaned closer until his lips were almost touching hers, and she closed her eyes. His hand moved to the back of her head, and he threaded his fingers in her hair before pulling her to him.

His kiss was tender and sweet. She fought the urge to kiss him back, but it was a lost cause. She parted her lips, and he wasted no time in deepening the kiss. His other hand roamed down her back and stopped just above her waistband. Then, he pressed into her, showing her just how much he wanted her. She moaned, and he pulled back to look at her.

She slowly opened her eyes at the loss of contact and noticed he was intensely studying her face. His expression was serious, and it made her anxious. His fingers were making small circles over the skin on her back, and his other hand was still in her hair.

"You said you had something to say?"

His mouth was set in a grim line, and she was afraid he wasn't going to answer—or maybe she was afraid he would. Both prospects were causing her some apprehension.

He finally let out a small sigh. "Do me a favor. Next time you decide you need some time, talk to me first. Please. I'll give you whatever time you need. Just don't scare me like that again."

Jane felt guilty. She sincerely hadn't meant to worry him. In all honesty, she hadn't thought he'd be overly concerned over her absence. Obviously, she was wrong. That knowledge made her stomach do little somersaults, but she knew better than to read too much into it. Tamping down her elation, she kept her expression indifferent.

She inhaled a shaky breath. "Okay."

He continued to look at her.

She started to become self-conscious. "What? Why do you keep looking at me like that?"

He moved his hand from her back and brought it to her face, his fingertips gently outlining her face from her temple to her chin. This time, it was his turn to inhale an unsteady breath.

"I just..." He swallowed, fighting to find the right words. "I can't go through that again. Brett and I looked everywhere. When the storm passed, we spent the entire night searching. I thought I'd lost you forever."

Colt's emotional wall dropped long enough for Jane to see and feel the pain he was experiencing. Her instinct was to comfort him. She closed her eyes and pulled him to her until their foreheads touched. When she opened her eyes, a tear broke loose and rolled down her cheek.

Colt reached up to wipe it away. "Damn. Don't cry, sweetheart. It's gonna be okay." He paused for a moment. "You and I...we're gonna be okay. I promise."

She shook her head. "I want to believe you, Colt, but we can't be sure about the future."

"You might be right, but I prefer to be optimistic." He reached down and put his arm under her knees before lifting her off the floor. "I do know that we have today. Let me show you how important today is. Let me give you that."

He carried her to a small bedroom down the hall and kicked open the door. He entered and then wasted no time in getting to the bed. He placed her on her back and then covered her body with his own.

Jane had all these amazing and terrifying powers, but nothing she was capable of could protect her from her need for Colt. She was defenseless against his touch. At that moment, she would follow him to the ends of the earth, but she prayed it would never come to that.

Dr. Weston had finished with his last appointment and was looking over his notes when his secretary called his office phone.

"Doctor, there's a George Daniels here to see you."

"Does he have an appointment?"

"No, sir. He says he needs to discuss a personal matter."

Dr. Weston frowned. He didn't recognize the name, so he had no idea what this man could want with him. He decided he'd never know if he didn't talk to the man.

"Okay, Terri. Send him on back."

He put down the phone and quickly put away the last of the patient records he'd been reviewing. A knock at the door signaled that his strange visitor had arrived.

"Come in."

A tall, thin man entered the room. He had a touch of gray at the temples and along his hairline. He smiled warmly at Dr. Weston. "I'm sorry to intrude so late in the day, doctor. If I could have waited until tomorrow, I would have."

Dr. Weston motioned for him to take a seat. "No, not a problem at all, Mr. Daniels. How can I help you? My secretary said it was a personal matter."

"Indeed it is. You see, I've heard rumors about a special young lady who recently arrived in the area. I'm hoping it's my daughter. Her name is Alice Daniels."

Dr. Weston applied his best poker face as he worked to learn more. "Your daughter? Hmm…I can't say for sure. What does she look like? How old is she?"

"Oh my. You can't miss her. She's twenty-two and taller than average, and she has the most gorgeous red hair you've ever seen." George paused for a moment, seeming a little nervous. "Also, she's very, uh…gifted."

Dr. Weston couldn't hold back his surprise. This man did seem to know about Jane. "Gifted how?"

George looked him in the eyes. "You'll think I'm crazy."

"Try me, Mr. Daniels."

"She can do things…things other people, normal people, can't do. When I heard the rumors, I was hoping I'd finally found her at last."

Dr. Weston smiled at him. "Do you happen to have a photo?"

George looked a little embarrassed and pulled a worn photo from his wallet. "Well, sort of. I have one from when she was a little girl. She was taken from us when she was twelve, so I don't have anything more recent."

"Taken? As in, kidnapped?"

"Yes, sir. We've been looking for her all these years. I'm trying not to get too excited. But like I said, the rumors I've heard make me think it could be her."

Dr. Weston stood up. "I'm so sorry to hear you lost your daughter, Mr. Daniels. I assure you, I'll do some asking around and see what we can learn. Is there a number where I can reach you?"

George wrote his number down on a slip of paper and handed it to Dr. Weston. "Thank you so much, doctor. You'll never know how much your help means to me. I've missed her so much, and with her mother gone…" He cleared his throat. "Well, it'd just be nice to have her back in my life."

Dr. Weston clapped George on the back and walked him to the door. "I'll contact you soon, Mr. Daniels. Keep the faith that you will find her."

George nodded and walked away, looking slightly dejected.

Dr. Weston waited until he pulled away and then rushed back to his office, writing down everything the man had said.

Jane was a kidnap victim?

That certainly might explain some things. When she had first been brought in, her injuries and health status had indicated possible abuse, but because she couldn't remember anything, there had been little recourse. Now that he possibly had some backstory on her and her real name, she might be able to piece the truth back together.

The man claiming to be her father had seemed to know a lot about her, and he'd had that picture of a child who resembled Jane remarkably. He had also known about her specific gifts.

Dr. Weston felt sure that had to count for something. Maybe the man knew how to help her. Those very gifts could be the reason she had been taken from him in the first place.

He ran all the possible scenarios through his head, and then decided the best course of action would be to just call Colt. Hopefully, he'd located Jane, and he could pass on this newest information. If she decided she wanted to contact George Daniels, Dr. Weston would give her the cell number. If she didn't feel comfortable meeting or talking to this stranger, then the man would never be the wiser.

Dr. Weston turned off the lights and bid his secretary good night as she finished shutting down her computer. He let her lock up as he loaded a large box of research papers into his car. He'd been dying to dive into these, especially since meeting Jane. Tonight, he hoped that he could finally sit down and learn something. His colleagues were studying telekinesis and various other phenomena in a private facility upstate. Maybe they could give some insight into what Jane was dealing with.

FOURTEEN

Colt was just waking up when he heard his cell phone ringing. He reached over to the nightstand and hit the Accept button.

As he rubbed the sleep from his face, he answered in a husky voice, "Hello?"

"Colt, it's Dr. Weston. Have you found Jane?"

Colt looked to his right. Jane was asleep on her stomach, her hair pulled to one side, exposing her bare back to him.

He smiled. "Yeah, Doc. I found her yesterday. Sorry. I should have called you. We just got busy, and it slipped my mind." He intended to replay their *busy* day every chance he got. Each time he touched her was like feeding an addiction—one he never wanted to overcome.

"Listen, Colt, something has happened. A man showed up, claiming to be her father."

That got his attention. He sat upright, letting the sheet fall to his waist. "No kidding. Do you think he's legit?"

"I'm not sure. He gave me some interesting but disturbing details, including her real name."

Colt looked at the woman lying next to him. "So, she might finally get the answers she's been looking for."

"Possibly. I didn't say I knew her, only that I'd keep an eye out. He gave me his number in case I heard anything. I thought it would be best for Jane to make this decision."

"Agreed." Colt continued to watch her sleep as he let the news sink in.

"I'll text you the info he gave me. You two can discuss it from there. If she wants me there, I'm happy to be a mediator. Just let me know."

"Thanks, Doc. I know she appreciates it."

"Keep me posted, Colt."

Dr. Weston hung up, and Colt placed his phone back on the nightstand.

He had an odd feeling about this family business. Something in his gut told him to be careful, but that wasn't his call. He hoped Jane would feel it, too, and not rush into anything. He reached over and lightly ran his fingers across the back of her neck, brushing away a couple of stray strands of her hair. Then, he leaned over and placed a warm kiss at the base of her neck. She stirred for a moment, so he continued to shower soft kisses down her back. She stretched and rolled over to see him hovering over her.

Jane smiled. "Mmm...I haven't slept that well in days." She looked out the window. "Is it morning already?"

Colt kissed her on the lips and then settled next to her, his head resting on his hand. "Yes, it's morning. You're welcome by the way."

"I am? What am I welcome for exactly?"

"The amazing sleep."

"And just how was that your doing?"

He gave her a wicked grin. "I satisfied your every need and completely wore you out."

She rolled her eyes. "Yes, I'm sure it was that and not the fact that I've spent the last couple of nights essentially camping out in the forest."

He stretched out on his back and put his hands behind his head. "Never underestimate the value of a good roll in the hay."

She laughed. "I'll remember that." Then, she sat up and swung her legs over the edge of the bed. "I'll also remember that you have a colossal ego."

As she stood, Colt's arms grabbed her, pulling her backward. He was pressed against her back—one arm securing her to him, the other reaching around to roam her body.

He whispered in her ear, "Admit it. You like my colossal...ego."

She laughed again and tried to push away, but he held his grip.

"Colt, I need to get up."

He growled in her ear, "So do I."

"Oh, dear God...I can't even have a simple conversation with you without it turning sexual."

He shrugged. "You're the one saying all the dirty stuff." Then, he laughed and let her go.

She threw a pillow at him and then shut herself in the bathroom.

He sat on the bed and contemplated their next move. He grabbed his phone again and scanned the text message Dr. Weston had sent. He supposed the next step would be to meet this Mr. Daniels, assuming Jane was even interested.

Deep down, he knew she would be. The possibility of knowing her identity and having a family connection would be too great a pull to ignore.

He'd just have to ensure he was by her side, giving her whatever support she needed each step of the way.

She exited the bathroom and grabbed her clothes from the nearby armchair. As she started to dress, Colt gathered his own clothes.

Once they were both dressed, he pulled her into a hug. "Are you hungry?"

"Famished."

"I'll make breakfast."

Colt busied himself with mixing pancakes and frying sausage. Jane watched, hoping to learn something about cooking since her skills were nonexistent. He enlisted her help, insisting she would learn by doing. In no time, they had a warm meal before them. She attacked her breakfast with enthusiasm and spent part of the meal declaring that pancakes were officially her favorite food.

After they cleaned up, Colt led her to the sofa. "I might have some news. I don't know if it's good or bad yet, but it's a possible lead to your past."

Jane's eyes went wide. "Really?" She'd almost given up on finding information about the person she used to be.

"Doc called this morning. He met a man claiming to know who you are."

She smiled. "That's amazing!"

He didn't seem as enthused. She figured this was where the bad news would come in.

"What's the catch?" she asked.

"No catch. Maybe a complication. Maybe not. It might be a great thing, sweetheart. I just don't know yet."

"So? Don't keep me in suspense!"

"He claims to be your father."

Jane stared at him in disbelief. "My father?" She wondered if it were actually possible. She didn't consider herself a fortunate person, and this almost seemed too good to be true.

Colt gave her hand a squeeze. "You don't have to meet him, if you aren't comfortable. Doc didn't tell him you were here. He just said he'd keep an eye out for you. That way, you could make the decision to meet this man or not."

She nodded, seeing the logic in Dr. Weston's judgment. "I appreciate his thoughtfulness." She twisted her fingers together as she considered her options. Looking up at Colt, she nodded. "I need to meet him. Nothing says I have to have further contact with him, but I at least need to try."

Colt attempted a smile to encourage her, but he was struggling to make it look genuine. He wasn't sure what he was worried about. It was just a meeting after all. But his gut twisted at the prospect. He considered the possibility that he was just being selfish. He liked having her to himself, and he'd never been too good at sharing anything that meant something to him. It was entirely plausible that he was afraid her family would take her away from him or warn her against him. It wouldn't be the first time a concerned father stepped in to keep his daughter from falling in love with Colt.

He shook off his doubts. He was determined to be happy for her, regardless of the outcome. "When do you want to meet him? Doc said he could set it up, or we could call Mr. Daniels directly."

"Mr. Daniels. My last name is Daniels?"

"So he claims. Alice Daniels, to be exact."

She let the name roll off her tongue a couple of times. It felt right. It felt familiar, yet she wasn't ready to claim it. "Let's stick with Jane for now."

"There are some other things you need to know about. They aren't all good."

She inhaled a deep breath. "Okay. Well, let's set up the meeting for tomorrow, somewhere public. That will give me time to let all this new information sink in. I'll do this one step at a time. Until then, I have something I need to show you. And I need to find my backpack."

Colt gave her a questioning look.

She explained further, "I hid it in a log near an area where I set up camp. I overexerted myself and woke up in the hospital. The two guys who found me didn't know about the pack, so I need to go back and get it."

"Overexerted? What two guys?"

Jane gave him an exasperated look. "The short version is that I passed out, and two hikers found me and took me to the emergency room. I woke up and didn't want to be there, so I left. That was when Lance found me, and we got something to eat. You know the rest."

At the mention of Lance, Jane noticed a muscle twitching in Colt's jaw. *Silly man. Can't he see I only have eyes for him?*

"Anyway, something amazing happened while I was gathering my thoughts out there. I want to show you."

She grabbed his hand and pulled him toward the front door. He grabbed his keys off an entry table as they passed it, and then he locked up behind them. She walked toward the bike while fashioning her hair into a quick braid to avoid the tangles she'd battled the previous evening.

Colt hesitantly followed but seemed less than enthused about the upcoming trip.

"C'mon, big guy. I promise, you'll like this surprise."

He sat on the motorcycle and waited for her to climb up behind him. Once she was settled, he started the engine.

"So, where do we find the backpack and your surprise?"

"It's just off of one of the trails not far from your cabin."

He sighed. "Seriously? I looked there. How did I miss you?"

She laughed. "I wasn't there until early yesterday. I was slowly making my way back."

He shook his head in disbelief, raised the kickstand with his boot, and pulled out of the driveway.

Jane spent the next forty-five minutes watching the scenes change from town to country and back again. When they pulled onto the familiar dirt road leading to Colt's cabin, she couldn't help but think of how this was where it had all started for them. She smiled at the thought of Colt taking care of her even though he hadn't known her at the time. Now, look at where they were. It seemed poetic in a strange way.

Arriving at the cabin, Colt went inside for a couple of bottles of water. He handed one to Jane. "Lead the way."

"Thank you." She smiled at him.

It was very much like the smiles he remembered from when he'd first met her. It was full of sunshine and vibrancy. Somewhere along the way, she'd lost that, and he was glad to see it had returned.

He reached out and caressed her jaw. "I missed that smile."

She blushed a little as she stepped forward and put her arms around his neck. She softly kissed him and then stepped back. "This way."

She led the way down one of the lesser-traveled paths, but after about half a mile, she veered off between some bushes and followed a trail that only she seemed to see. Colt followed behind, hoping she knew where she was going. It wasn't long before she was jogging toward a large log near a small clearing.

"Here it is!" She pulled the backpack from the hollow log and dusted it off.

"Great. Glad you found it." He looked around. "So, what's this surprise you keep talking about?"

She absentmindedly waved a hand at him as she faced the clearing. "So impatient."

He grinned but said nothing.

She smirked and motioned for him to come closer. He stepped next to her.

She pointed to the clearing in front of them. "What do you see?"

He looked puzzled. "I see weeds and grass."

"What would you like to see?"

He looked at her. "You. Naked. In my bed."

She gave him a playful shove. "No, not that. I mean, in the field. What is your favorite flower?"

He raised an eyebrow at her. "I'm pretty sure I'd get my balls confiscated if I actually had a favorite flower—man code and all."

"Ugh. You are so frustrating! Fine. Name a flower, any flower."

Colt had no idea what she was getting at, but he'd humor her. He named the first thing he could think of, "Dandelion."

"Dandelion? That's a weed, too, Colt."

"Hey, it has color and petals and crap."

She rolled her eyes. "Fair enough. Now, watch."

She closed her eyes and allowed joy and life to fill her thoughts and her heart. The colors in her mind swirled until they resembled a field of yellow. She opened her eyes and raised one hand in front of her. Squatting down, she touched the earth and let the emotion flow through her fingertips.

Colt's eyes widened as he watched dandelions sprouting from the ground, starting at Jane's fingers and making their way through the clearing until the entire area looked like a landscaper's nightmare.

Jane stood and turned to him, beaming with pride.

He slowly looked back to her. "How in the hell?"

She giggled with an almost giddy excitement.

"But…" He was speechless. Then, a wide grin replaced his confusion. "You did it? You figured it out?"

She nodded her head. "I did! It took lots of practice, but I'm learning to use these gifts for something other than destroying things and scaring or hurting people."

He picked her up and swung her around. "That's fantastic!"

He kissed her soundly. "But remember, those other times, you were protecting yourself. That's not a bad thing."

"I know, but I couldn't control it. Now, I can—for the most part anyway."

He wrapped his arms around her tighter. "So, what else can you do?"

She smiled sheepishly. "I can sorta control the weather."

"No damn way!"

"Not in big ways. Just little things. Like the night it rained so badly? I was able to keep dry, thanks to some very accommodating clouds."

He looked at her with amazement. "I'm proud of you for not giving up. I'm sorry I assumed you were running from your problems."

"To be honest, at first, I was. But once I got out here, my curiosity overcame my fear."

"Speaking of curiosity and fear, we should get back to the cabin and call Doc to set up that meeting."

She nodded and then turned to grab her backpack. Colt picked it up before she had the chance, and he slung it over his shoulder. With his other hand, he grasped hers. They walked, hand in hand, toward the path and back to the cabin.

At ten the next morning, Jane and Colt sat on a park bench, waiting for Dr. Weston to arrive with the mysterious Mr. Daniels. Jane was once again twisting her fingers, letting her nerves get the better of her. Colt placed a hand over hers to still her busy fingers.

"I'm right here, beautiful. Nothing is going to happen that you don't want to happen."

She nodded in agreement but didn't seem to relax at all.

"Besides, if he turns out to be a dirtbag, you can zap him with your powers and turn him into a toad."

She couldn't help but laugh. "I'm not a witch, Colt." She thought about it for a moment longer. "Am I? Don't witches use spells and stuff?"

Colt smiled at her. "I haven't the foggiest idea. I've never met one."

"Me neither. I didn't believe they even existed, but now, I wonder."

She didn't have time to expound on it further. Dr. Weston and a tall man who looked to be in his fifties approached their bench.

"Jane and Colt, I'd like to introduce Mr. George Daniels. Mr. Daniels, this is Jane and Colt Henderson."

Mr. Daniels raised his eyebrows in surprise. "Jane and Colt Henderson? Are you married?"

Dr. Weston gave a nervous laugh. "Oh, dear. I'm so sorry. I bungled that introduction. Let me try again." He gestured to Colt. "This is Colt Henderson. He's a good friend of Jane's." Then, he presented Jane. "This is Jane, the young lady I was telling you about."

George shook Jane's hand and warmly smiled at her. "My dear girl, it's so very nice to see you."

Jane looked at the man before her, and a small spark of recognition registered somewhere in her subconscious. "It's nice to meet you, Mr. Daniels."

Colt stood and offered his hand as well. When George placed his hand in Colt's grasp, he felt his strength and the underlying message Colt was sending him. Colt expected him to be exactly who he'd said he was, or he'd face the consequences. He gave Colt an acknowledging nod and then stepped back.

George cleared his throat. "I know this is unconventional, but would it be possible for me to speak with my daughter—I mean, Miss Jane alone for a few minutes?"

Colt started to step between them, but Jane placed a hand on his arm.

"It's okay, Colt. We'll go sit at that table over there. I promise, we'll stay in sight."

Colt didn't like it at all, but he knew that Jane had to do what she thought was necessary.

"I'll be right here, watching. If anything looks off, I'm coming over there."

Dr. Weston, in his effort to be her champion as well, chimed in, "Me, too!"

She squeezed Colt's arm and smiled at Dr. Weston. Then, she walked to the nearby picnic table with the man she thought to be her father.

She was acutely aware of George's mannerisms, noting that each gesture felt familiar. Even the inflection in his voice seemed to register with her in a way she couldn't explain.

He pulled a photo from his shirt pocket and passed it across to her.

"This is a photo of my daughter, Alice, when she was around twelve. I assume Dr. Weston explained my situation to you?"

"Yes, he did." She studied the photo, familiar eyes staring back at her from the worn paper. Her hand shook. "Oh God."

George looked concerned and reached for her other hand. "Are you okay?"

She dropped the photo and clamped her hand over her mouth. Out of the corner of her eye, she saw Colt stalking toward them. She waved him away, assuring him all was fine. He stopped, unsure if he should continue forward or turn around. He watched her for a moment and then walked back to Dr. Weston.

She looked at George. "I'm okay. She just looks like someone I know." She wasn't about to tell him that Alice was the little girl in her visions. She wasn't ready to disclose that information to a stranger, father or not.

He gazed at her and smiled. "She looks like you. I know this all seems crazy. Dr. Weston told me you had no memories of your life before your accident, but I can feel it in my heart. You are Alice Daniels."

She looked at him, wide-eyed and conflicted. A part of her really wanted to believe him. Another part wanted to run and forget she'd ever met him. She didn't know which to trust.

He sighed. "Listen, it's a lot to adjust to at once. Take some time to think. Ask me any questions you might have. If you decide you aren't Alice, I'll leave you alone. But if even a tiny part of you feels recognition, please allow me to try to reconcile—on your terms, of course."

She nodded. "Sounds fair." She thought for a moment. "Can I ask you a question?"

He nodded. "Anything."

"You told Dr. Weston that your daughter was gifted. What did you mean by that?"

He appeared uncomfortable with the question. "It's hard to explain. But if you really are Alice, you probably already know."

She expectantly looked at him.

"It began when she was about six. She would get upset, and things would happen, things we didn't understand. It started small—her toys flying across the room and such—but as she grew, so did the strength of her abilities. Before long, she could move large pieces of furniture or levitate items in the air, all without ever physically touching them."

He realized Jane was listening intently, so he continued, "Once she was old enough to understand that she was special, she became scared. We hired some top-notch researchers to help us understand what was happening. We wanted to help her embrace her gifts, not to fear them. She worked with them for several years before"—his voice cracked, and he closed his eyes— "someone bad caught wind of the research being done. We tried to keep her hidden from those who would abuse her abilities, but they eventually found us."

He rubbed the bridge of his nose. "They broke in one night and took Alice by force. My wife was killed, trying to protect her. I was knocked unconscious. I haven't seen her since." He pulled a handkerchief from the pocket of his trousers and swiped at his eyes.

She reached across the picnic table for his hand, hoping to give him comfort, undeterred by the fact that she was reeling from these revelations. She was starting to believe that she really was Alice Daniels. The gifts and the visions of what must have been her childhood—or at least part of it— seemed to fit with what Mr. Daniels was describing. Some of her visions had been completely terrifying. She wasn't sure she wanted to remember. But if she'd been kidnapped, it also explained why most of the dreams and visions had scared her.

He accepted her gesture of kindness and squeezed her hand. "Sweet little Alice…she always loved to help me. I remember one time, we were in the garage, and she was trying to help me build a birdhouse. We cut and placed all the pieces on the workbench. In her excitement to get the hammer, she knocked a glass of lemonade off the table, and it shattered. The bottom half of the glass was still intact and lying on its side on the floor. The noise had startled her so badly that she inadvertently ran into it, cutting a deep half-circle gash into her ankle. She had to get several stitches, but she was such a brave girl."

Jane looked down at her own ankle, the faint half-circle scar still evident, despite her pale complexion. Blurred images of her childhood raced through her mind. They still weren't clear enough that she could tell what was what, but she felt the evidence was too obvious to overlook.

Tears welled in her eyes as she ran around the table and threw herself into his arms. "Oh, Daddy!"

He hugged her back. "My Alice! My dear sweet Alice! I'm so very glad I've found you!"

FIFTEEN

NOW APPROACHES THE MOMENT I'VE WAITED FOR.

MY STRUGGLES ARE NEARING AN END.

Watching from a distance as Jane embraced George, Colt wanted to believe this was a good thing, but he was still struggling to accept it.

Dr. Weston nudged him in the ribs. "Isn't it exciting, boy? We've reunited a family!"

"Yeah, it's great, Doc."

"You don't sound convinced. Why?"

"I dunno. I'm just tired, I guess."

Dr. Weston clapped him on the back. "Well, I have another bit of good news for you. Jerry never actually filed those assault charges. He was just blowing steam. Yesterday, he was arrested himself for the same thing." He frowned. "Lisa's in pretty bad shape this time. I hope she doesn't drop the charges."

Colt fumed, "I knew that dickweed was hitting her. Will she be okay?"

"I'm sure she will, if she follows my orders to take it easy once she's discharged." He observed Jane and her father interacting, and he smiled. "And you can come home without worrying about being arrested."

"Thanks, Doc."

Colt noticed Dr. Weston glancing at his watch. "Got somewhere to be? I can handle it from here if you need to go."

Dr. Weston looked embarrassed. "Well, I do have some rounds to do at the hospital. I planned to go in later, but since things seem to be shaping up rather well here…do you mind if I leave?"

"Go on, Doc. I got it."

Dr. Weston called out to Jane, and they waved good-bye before he hurried to his car.

Her eyes met Colt's.

As always, when Colt looked at her, a spark seemed to travel through the air, landing right in his chest. She smiled, and he couldn't help but return it. She looked happy, and that made him happy.

Colt settled himself on the nearby bench and tried to be patient while father and daughter caught up. He suddenly felt like a third wheel, but there was no way he would leave her alone with him. He would stay, no matter how long they decided to talk.

Luckily for him, it was only another ten minutes or so before they stood and walked in his direction.

Jane clasped Colt's hand in hers and smiled up at her father. "I know you've been introduced already, but I just want you to know that Colt is an important part of my life."

Colt's heart swelled at the admission she was making in front of her father. He smiled at George, and George smiled back, but Colt got the impression that the smile wasn't genuine. He once again had to remind himself that this was about Jane—*or would it be Alice now?* He wasn't sure how long it would take him to get used to that.

George gave her a hug. "I'm going to my hotel. Call me tomorrow maybe?"

She nodded, and he walked toward the parking lot, not even sparing Colt a backward glance.

Jane threw her arms around Colt and hugged him to her. "Isn't it wonderful? I have family!"

Colt smiled down at her and then kissed her forehead. "It's amazing, sweetheart, simply amazing." He looked back to where George had been walking, but he was already gone. "I'm not sure he approves of me so much though."

She frowned. "Why do you think that?"

"Eh, just a hunch. I'm not the kind of guy you usually bring home to meet the folks."

"Don't be silly. If that's the case, he'll just have to learn to love you as much as I do." Jane closed her eyes as she realized the word *love* had slipped out before she could stop it. She'd wondered many times if what she was feeling for him was love, but she'd never expected to admit it so soon. She fought down the rising panic in her chest.

Maybe I'm lucky enough that he didn't hear me. I should just play it off as no big deal.

She opened her eyes to see Colt giving her an unsettling stare that seemed to see through to her soul. It scared and excited her at the same time.

He raised his hand to her face and stroked his index finger from her cheekbone to her jawline. "You said you love me."

Oh God, he did hear me. "Listen, Colt, you don't have to—"

116

He interrupted her, "Did you mean it?"

She couldn't lie to him, especially not about this. "Yes," she said quietly.

He picked her up and practically ran to his motorcycle.

She clung to his neck and laughed. "What are you doing?"

"Getting you home as quickly as possible."

She was confused. "Why?"

"Because I can't say it back, Jane."

She tried to hide the pain those words had induced. She was almost sure he could audibly hear her heart breaking.

Colt set her down in front of the motorcycle and then lifted her chin to meet his face. "I can't say it back because I'm not sure the word *love* could do justice to my feelings for you. But I can show you. I can take you home and spend the rest of the day showing you what you mean to me."

Her heart went from shattering to inflating in the span of a few seconds. It was almost dizzying.

Jane smiled at him, holding back the happy tears threatening to fall. "Show me then."

The next week went by in a blur. Jane would spend part of her days with George, getting reacquainted with a man she barely remembered. The rest of her time was spent with Colt.

Colt returned to Mike's Bikes, expecting a lukewarm welcome, but he learned that Mike and Macy had kept their mouths shut about the incident with Jane. They were more than happy to have him back. With Jerry gone, Mike was in dire need of his best mechanic, and he offered Colt a raise to stay. Colt agreed with the stipulation that he set his own hours for the time being.

Jane was feeling optimistic about her future. While Colt was still cautious in regard to her father, he was open and loving to her. She felt worshiped and adored when she was with him.

She was also learning from her father about the methods she'd used to control her gifts as a child. It seemed that while she had practiced in the forest, old habits had kicked in and helped her along. George seemed especially proud of her upon hearing that she could once again keep her abilities on a leash. He never belittled her or made her feel like a freak about her gifts.

The only thing she was struggling with was his need to address her as Alice. Instinctively, she knew that was her name, but she just couldn't seem to adjust to using it. She allowed him to call her Alice, but she preferred that everyone else continued to call her Jane. She was still figuring out who Alice was, and until that happened, she needed breathing room.

Saturday morning, Jane was sitting in the park with George, watching the children play. He told her story after story of her childhood. He described her favorite toys, her playmates, and her utter adoration for orange sherbet. She laughed and asked questions, generally enjoying her time with him.

A little girl ran by them, giggling and jumping, when she tripped on her shoelace and skinned her knee. She looked to be only four or five years of age, and her brunette pigtails bobbed up and down as she sobbed into her hands.

Jane ran to the little girl to reassure her that all would be okay. "Hey, sweetheart. What's your name?"

The girl pulled in a huge gulp of air and tried not to cry. "M-m-my name i-is Li-Lindy."

"It's nice to meet you, Lindy. My name is Jane. May I look at your knee?"

Lindy bushed the tears from her eyes and then used her shirt to wipe her nose. "O-okay."

Jane sat down on the sidewalk next to her. Lindy extended her knee and winced. The scrapes weren't deep, but they were red and bleeding a little.

Lindy saw the blood and started sobbing again. "Am I-I-I gonna d-die?" She started to hiccup between sobs.

"Oh no, Lindy. You're gonna be just fine. In fact, soon you'll be better than new."

Lindy looked up at Jane with big brown eyes. Tears framed her full dark lashes. "I'll b-be okay?"

"Yes, ma'am. In fact, I bet if you close your eyes and think happy thoughts, you'll forget all about this nasty fall. Should we try?"

Lindy tried to smile. "I want to try."

"Good. Here's what we'll do. You hold my hand and close your eyes."

Lindy did as instructed, squeezing her eyes as tightly as she could.

Jane smiled at this beautiful little girl before her and then closed her eyes as well. "Now, Lindy, tell me about things you like. It can be anything that makes you happy."

Lindy scrunched up her face as she thought of her favorite things. Then, she produced a wide smile, exposing a cute little gap between her front teeth. "My puppy! His name is Boots, and he is so soft and fuzzy. He licks my face, and he barks when I come home and..." Lindy took a big breath. "and he loves to sleep on my bed and I give him my broccoli 'cause I don't like it."

Jane couldn't help but laugh. "Boots sounds like a wonderful puppy! What color is he?"

Lindy started to describe her puppy in great detail, including his spots and how he sometimes peed on the floor. While she described the dog, Jane took a minute to let the joyful colors swirl in her mind, hoping to transfer some of that joy to little Lindy. If she could take away some of this child's pain, she'd be glad for all she'd experienced leading up to this moment.

"Hey!" Lindy released Jane's hand and clapped them together.

Jane opened her eyes, happy that her joy had transferred to this sweet child. What she hadn't expected to see was the child's knee was now scrape-free.

Jane looked stunned.

The little girl stood and then bounced up and down. She hugged Jane and gave her a slobbery kiss on her cheek. "Thank you for helping me, Jane! I'm all better now!"

Jane reached down to tie the little girl's shoes, so she wouldn't trip again while she worked hard not to inspect her knee a second time, just to be sure she wasn't imagining things. "I'm glad you feel better, Miss Lindy. Now, always make sure your shoes are tied before you run, okay?"

Lindy nodded.

"Is your mommy here?"

Lindy frowned. "No, she's at work. I'm here with Candice. She's my babysitter." She pointed to a teen who was totally immersed in whatever was on her smartphone. She sat on a bench halfway across the park and seemed completely oblivious to anything around her, including her charge.

"Can you do me a favor, Lindy?"

Lindy nodded once again.

"Please stay close to Candice, okay? You will be safe that way. Promise?"

Lindy seemed to consider that. "Okay, but the swings are over here."

Jane patted her on the back. "Then, you should go tell Candice you need her to push you on the swings. Ask her to help you, okay?"

Lindy smiled and ran off toward Candice.

Behind her, George was watching intently. He didn't say a word, but she could tell by his expression that he was just as astonished by this new revelation.

He cleared his throat. "You have quite a way with kids."

A nervous laugh escaped her lips as she moved to sit next to him again. "Yeah, I guess you could say that."

He frowned. "Has that ever happened before? The healing, I mean?"

"No. That's new."

He nodded his understanding but looked worried. "Could we have dinner tonight? There's something I'd like to discuss with you."

"Sure. You could come to Colt's house, and we'll cook."

He shook his head. "I think it's best if you and I discuss this alone. It's not that I don't like Colt. He seems like a great guy. But this is a sensitive subject, and I'd feel better if we discussed it before we talked to anyone else about it."

She didn't see the harm in having Colt present, but maybe George was right. *What if it was something horrible that she wouldn't want Colt to know? What if it was something from her past?* "Can't we just talk now?"

"I need to make some phone calls first. I…please, Alice. Just trust me on this. It's best to keep this between you and me for now." He pulled her in for a hug. "I lost you all those years ago, and I want to be sure it never happens again." He looked into her eyes. "I'm just trying to keep you safe. Bad people are still out there."

His meaning slowly sank in.

"Are they looking for me? The people who took me?" she asked.

His grim expression said all she needed to know.

"Now that I think about it, we should include Colt. He needs to know what we are up against. So, I'll take you up on that offer to cook, if it still stands."

"Sure. Drop by around six thirty or so, and we'll talk."

George gave her a final hug and then cupped her chin in his hands. "My girl. Just look at you. My heart swells with pride at the woman you've become."

She smiled at him. "Thanks, Dad."

Colt sat the table as he listened to Jane singing softly in the next room. She'd been humming one tune or another all afternoon. Despite her nervousness over her father's upcoming visit, she'd been overjoyed that she had helped little Lindy in such a major way.

He stood and pulled a casserole out of the oven and then placed it next to a large salad bowl on the table.

Jane smiled at him as she walked into the kitchen. She finished putting the back on one earring and then pulled her hands away. "How do I look?"

He slowly looked her over, starting at her head and purposefully making his way down. He raised his eyes to hers. "You have way too many clothes on."

"Colt, seriously, how do I look? I don't know why, but I'm nervous."

He walked to her and pulled her into his arms. "You look beautiful, sweetheart. You always look beautiful." He kissed her and was about to take his seduction a little further when the doorbell rang. "Damn. Saved by the bell."

She smiled at him and moved to answer the door.

When she opened it, George walked in with a bouquet of flowers in his hand. "These are for you, dearest."

She touched the flowers, but suddenly, she was no longer in Colt's living room.

Jane looked around to find herself in a small room. It would have been a somewhat cheerful area if bars weren't on the windows. She frowned. Then, she heard a familiar voice.

"You came back. We hoped you would."

Jane spun around to see the red-haired girl from her other visions. She noted that she was actually looking at a younger version of herself. This version was a little older— maybe sixteen or seventeen—and she looked tired and pale.

"What's going on, Alice? Why am I here? Why are you here?"

"They took us, all of us. And we can't be free until you come back for us."

Jane shook her head. "No. This makes no sense. I am free now."

Younger Alice sadly looked at her. "Not yet, you aren't."

Then, she heard a man's voice behind her.

"What happened?" he asked.

Jane froze for a moment, afraid to turn around. As she gathered the courage to look at the man speaking behind her, she felt arms wrapping around her.

"Dearest, speak to me! Open your eyes!"

Jane blinked. Colt had his arms around her, and George was directly in front of her, trying to get her attention.

"Are you all right, Alice?" George's worried tone snapped her to attention.

She attempted to stand on her own, and Colt kept a hand on her for stability.

"Yeah, I'm fine. I just…" She looked at Colt. "I had another weird vision."

George's frown deepened. "You're having visions? Oh, dear, I was afraid this would happen."

Colt and Jane both stared at him, their worried expressions begging for an explanation.

George motioned to the couch. "You should sit down for this."

They moved to the couch.

George took the armchair. "Your gifts are remarkable, so remarkable that you belonged to a secret society called The Curators. They felt it was important to ensure that you and others like you were cared for and appreciated for your unique abilities. They wanted to foster your gifts without exposing you to the evils of the world."

He stood and rubbed the back of his neck. Then, he paced a couple of times before continuing, "You can imagine how difficult it was for a little girl with your special talents to attend a regular school without drawing attention to herself. So, we attended classes that taught you self-control. It wasn't long before you could attend school, make friends, and be like any other child your age. The difference was that you had a secret the other children knew nothing about, and you got very good at hiding it."

He walked to where Jane sat and crouched down in front of her. He took her hand. "Something went wrong, Alice. The man in charge decided the society needed to live up to its name. Instead of helping children like you, he started collecting them, keeping them like pieces in a museum. He'd spent years inserting like-minded henchmen into the organization. Those of us who fought back didn't stand a chance. We were outnumbered. He found a way to kill pretty much everyone who disagreed with his plan. "

He sighed. "Your mother and I took you and ran. At the time, there was nothing we could do for the other children, but we could keep you safe—at least, we thought we could."

His sad expression made her heart ache for him. She looked at Colt and saw that he was also hurting for the man before them.

"They broke in one night while we were reading together, and—"

Jane interrupted, "They stabbed Mother."

George looked confused. "Yes, they did. Do you remember? I'd hoped that particular memory wouldn't return."

She nodded. "I remember some of it. I saw it in a vision. You were making silly noises while we read." She paused to think. "Why were you making silly noises? I thought I was twelve when I was taken?"

He gave her a sad look. "You were. I was just being obnoxious. You were laughing at your stupid dad."

She smiled at the thought, but she wished she could remember more of her mother. In the vision, she seemed to be wonderful.

George's expression became grim once again. "These people are still out there. You somehow escaped, but they won't stop until they find you again. Of all the children, you were their most valued prize. And if they ever catch wind that your powers have expanded…to healing, they'd gladly kill anyone who got in their way of retrieving you."

He gave Colt a pointed look.

Colt frowned. He knew what George was getting at, and he didn't like it.

"What are you saying, Dad?"

"I'm saying that you aren't safe here. And Colt isn't safe if he's with you."

She turned to Colt, and he read the fear on her face.

His anger rose. "Hold on. There has to be a way I can help protect her. I'm not helpless, Mr. Daniels. I've kept her safe this far."

"I know, Colt, and you'll never know how much I appreciate that. But this is going to get complicated very quickly. These people are dangerous and capable of deeds you couldn't even imagine." He looked at Jane. "For now, the safest course is to come back with me. We have a facility that is serving as a refugee camp of sorts for those with your gifts."

She wiped away a tear. "How many others are like me?"

"Like you? None. So far, you are one of a kind. But there are others with similar gifts—mostly telekinesis. I've managed to find a few of the others who escaped over the years, and we are doing our best to help them in a way we couldn't before. I've never forgiven myself for abandoning all those children, but at the time, I saw no other way to ensure your safety. I'm trying to fix that mistake."

She looked at Colt. "He's making sense. Maybe I can help keep the others safe."

Colt stood up. "No! There has to be another way!" His panic was building rapidly.

"But, Colt, I can help!"

He flexed his fingers and glared at George. "I think you should leave. Jane and I need to talk."

George looked at her. "Jane? You're still using Jane?"

"I'm sorry. I'm just having a hard time adjusting to Alice. I'll get there."

Colt had to bite his tongue to keep from yelling at both of them. He walked to the front door and opened it.

George took the hint and made his way to the door. "Think about what I said, please. I'm not exaggerating when I say it's life or death."

He stepped out, and Colt slammed the door behind him.

Sixteen

Colt fumed. He knew he had no right to be angry with Jane. She was only trying to protect others, but it frustrated the hell out of him that she couldn't see the alternatives.

He walked back to where she stood and stuffed his hands in his pockets. He was afraid if he touched her, he'd drag her into the bedroom and never let her out.

She looked mad as well. "Colt, you had no right to throw my father out."

"The hell I didn't! It's my house. When someone comes in and tries to take what's mine, I fight for it!"

"Yours? Did you just say *yours*? I've told you before, Colt. I'm not an object to be owned."

"Damn it, I know that! That's not what I meant!"

"Could have fooled me. The moment it looks like I might choose something other than what you want, you freak out and start throwing a tantrum."

He shook his head. "So, I'm a toddler now, am I?"

"If the shoe fits…"

"Well, that's fair, coming from a coward."

She moved closer, leaving only a few inches separating them. Her voice pitched to a screech as she yelled, "A coward?"

"Yes, a coward!" He was now standing nose-to-nose with her. His voice was deadly calm. "When things get hard, you run."

"Did you ever think I was doing it for you, Colt? Did that ever cross your mind?"

"Yeah, I've heard that before."

"Colt, I already told you. I needed time to sort things out."

"Uh-huh. But you left a pretty final-sounding good-bye note. You weren't planning on coming back."

She sighed. "No, you're right. At that time, I wasn't going to return. I didn't know what I know now."

He reached for her, placing his hands on her hips. "And this is the same situation. There are other options. You don't have to go. I'll keep you safe. I'll help you win."

She fought back tears. "But who will keep you safe? I meant it when I said I loved you, Colt. I could never live with myself if something happened to you, especially if it happened because of me."

"I'm not helpless, Jane. I'm not without resources. Dr. Weston has been studying some research on the subject. He might already have found something helpful."

She closed her eyes and buried her head into his neck, wanting to change the subject. "Can we sleep on it? I can't think. It's just too much to take in."

Colt wanted to settle it now, but he knew pushing her wouldn't benefit either of them. And he was pretty sure she'd made up her mind the moment George told her others were in danger. "Sure. Let's get some rest."

She pulled back and looked into the kitchen. "We didn't eat. I'm sure the food is cold by now."

He shrugged. "I've lost my appetite anyway." He pulled away and went into the bedroom. He came out with a pillow and blanket. "I'll sleep in the spare room."

She frowned. "Colt, please, don't do this. There's no reason to."

Colt shook his head. "You needed space before. Now, it's my turn." He pushed open the door to the extra bedroom and stepped inside. "Good night...Alice." Then, he shut the door.

She stood rooted in place, wishing her powers included changing the past. There were so many things she'd like to fix.

Jane spent most of her night tossing and turning. It was amazing how quickly one could get used to having someone else in the bed. She'd doze off and dream of losing Colt, only to wake up and reach for him, knowing he wasn't there. Her dreams ranged from him finding another woman to a faceless group of people killing him in horrible ways. She'd woken up more than once with tears streaming down her face and various objects levitating around her.

She went through her regular morning routine, hoping to hear Colt stirring somewhere in the house. She needed to make him understand. This wasn't just about them. It was about so many others who, for whatever reason, were born with unusual abilities. She had to put her dreams aside for a while and focus on helping them. It didn't mean she could never see him, but it did mean she'd have to leave for a while.

She'd miss him terribly. Just the thought of being away from him made her chest ache. He was a part of her very soul. But in time, things would get better. They could be together again once this situation was sorted out. She truly believed that.

She walked into the living room and noticed that Colt was sitting in the armchair, drinking whiskey from the bottle.

She glanced at her watch. "Colt, it's not even nine yet. Why are you swigging that stuff so early?"

He glared at her and took another deliberate drink, as if to spite her. "Who cares what time it is?"

She looked closer and realized his eyes were bloodshot. "Did you sleep at all last night?"

He shrugged and then tossed something on the coffee table.

Her eyes widened when she realized it was a photo of him and his brother as children, and a vibrant-looking young woman was holding them. It was obviously a cherished picture, judging by the beautiful silver frame surrounding it. It didn't take her but a few seconds to realize that this must be his mother.

She stepped closer and noticed the similarities in their features. "Is this your mom?"

He didn't answer.

"Are you going to talk to me or just drink yourself to death?"

He stood up. "What difference does it make?"

"Colt! Stop this! We need to talk, and you need to be sober, so you'll understand."

He sneered at her. "I understand perfectly well. You're going to leave to protect others because you're unselfish that way. You always put others before yourself." His gaze softened. "It's one of the things I love about you. It's also one of the things I hate about you right now."

She clasped her hands in front of her and started to twist her fingers.

He noticed and ran a frustrated hand through his hair. "Just…go. Pack your stuff, and go."

Her heart was breaking as she watched this amazing, strong man slowly give up. "Colt, they need me right now."

"*They* need you? What about me? I need you more, damn it!" He threw the whiskey bottle, and it shattered against the wall.

Jane watched the amber liquid run down the wall, realizing her tears were echoing their movements. "I love you, Colt. I'll always love you," she said it so quietly that she wasn't sure he'd even heard her.

He picked up the photo of his mother and spent a moment gazing at it. He let out a disbelieving laugh. "She said she loved me, too. Then, she left and never came back." His eyes rose to meet Jane's. Tears were building on his lashes as he stared at her. He quickly swiped them away with the back of his hand.

His expression hardened. "Don't waste any time worrying about me. I'll be fine. Go save the world. I was wrong. I don't need you." He tossed the photo of his mom in the unused fireplace and walked past her, being careful not to touch her.

"Colt, please hear me out."

He opened the front door and kept going until he was on his motorcycle. He pulled out, his back tire squealing as he drove away. He couldn't get away from her and her damn emotional entanglements fast enough.

That afternoon, Jane packed her meager belongings in the backpack and carried them to her favorite park bench. She sat alone with her thoughts, wondering if she was making the right decision.

Her eyes were puffy and red from all the crying she'd done the last several hours. Colt's direct cut had hurt, but she knew he had just been reacting to his fear of being abandoned again. She didn't know how, but she hoped she could eventually make him see that she was nothing like his mother. She truly did love him, and someday, she'd find a way to prove it.

As she watched children playing on the slide, she recognized a familiar face.

He approached cautiously. "Hi. I don't know if you know who I am, but—"

She warily eyed him. "Yeah, I know who you are. Peter Grant, right? The guy on the news."

He nodded but looked afraid to come any closer. "Would you mind if we talked for a few minutes?"

She shrugged. "Why not? Have a seat." She moved her backpack, so he could sit next to her.

He perched himself on the edge of the bench, looking ready to bolt at any moment. "I've heard a lot about you. I know how rumors can get out of hand. I just wanted to possibly interview you, maybe get your side of things."

She raised her eyes to his. "Now really isn't a good time, Mr. Grant."

He took notice of her red-rimmed eyes. "Are you okay?"

She shook her head. "No, I'm not, but someday, I will be." She inhaled a deep breath. "As for your story, I'm sure you know that Jerry has had it in for my boy—" She stopped herself short. "For Colt for some time. And Jerry beats women. So, please excuse me if I refuse to give credence to any of the ridiculous rumors circulating about Colt or me." She sniffled and dabbed her eyes with the tissue she'd been clutching for the past half an hour.

"I'm truly sorry that Jerry has been causing you so much heartache, ma'am."

She glanced at the reporter and thought she saw sincerity in his eyes, but she was no longer sure she could trust her instincts.

"May I ask about Max and the incident in the bar? He told me what happened."

She pressed her lips together in a frustrated line. "Not much to tell. The town drunk attacked me in a restroom. I defended myself. Colt stepped in and helped me get away."

"So, that's all there was to it? He tells a much different story."

She let out an unladylike snort. "I'm sure he does. He's lucky that I don't prosecute for attempted rape. He's not about to tell the truth when he's the guilty party." She gave Peter a look that indicated she was done with the conversation. "Don't you have better things to report about, Mr. Grant? Like city corruption or domestic abuse? If you really want a story, go talk to Lisa Thompson about getting beaten by Jerry on a regular basis. Now, there's a problem people need to be aware of."

Peter had the decency to actually look ashamed. "I apologize for intruding, ma'am. I wish you well."

He stood and walked away, passing George as he left. Her dad gave Peter a strange look and then joined her on the bench.

"What was all that about?"

Jane shook her head. "Nothing important." She grabbed her backpack. "Are we ready to go?"

George took her hand in his. "You're doing the right thing, you know. I've seen how you look at Colt. If he's involved, he could get hurt. I know you'd feel guilty about that for the rest of your life. In time, things will work out for you both, but for now, we must do what we must do."

She tilted her head at him, nodding slowly. She repeated the phrase in her head, *We must do what we must do.*

It must be something he'd said often when she was a child because it seemed to ring a bell.

She stood.

George took her backpack. "This is everything?"

She nodded. "I haven't really had time to put down roots yet."

He gave her a slight hug. "That's for the best, I'm sure."

He placed his hand on the middle of her back and guided her to the parking area. When they neared a van he had pointed out to her, she noticed two men standing near it. She looked at George with a worried expression.

He smiled at her. "Alice, I'd like you to meet my friends Dennis and Robert. They came in case we run into any trouble along the way."

They both smiled at her.

She felt a familiarity regarding the two men. "Have we met before?"

They looked at each other and then to George.

He laughed. "Remember, boys? She's lost her memory of the past." He turned to her. "They worked with me for years, dearest. You practically grew up with them."

She felt silly. "Oh, so sorry. I hope to eventually remember everyone."

Dennis waved it off as nothing. "Don't let it bother you. We are just glad to have found you alive and well. It was quite a scare when you went missing."

She nodded. "I'm sure it was, especially since I was so young."

Dennis and Robert nodded in agreement.

Robert opened the back door of a small blue minivan. "We've taken the liberty of placing some comforts for you near the backseat. We thought you might want to rest or would like some snacks for the trip."

"Thank you. That was very kind." She climbed in and made herself comfortable in the back, buckling in and leaning against a large feather pillow.

The three men took their places in the vehicle with George near the back, so he could talk to her.

She closed her eyes as he talked about the facility and how well everyone was doing there. Before long, she drifted off to sleep, the exhaustion of her difficult morning taking over. She dreamed of Colt.

His greyish-blue eyes bored into hers as he pulled her close. She smiled and raised her hand to his face. She closed her eyes and let him kiss her. When she opened her eyes, it wasn't Colt kissing her, but some strange man she'd never seen before.

She screamed.

George woke her up. They had pulled over on the shoulder of the highway, and the driver, Dennis, appeared terrified. She looked around and realized her dream had caused a minor disturbance inside the van. Papers previously filed in a box were now scattered around the van as if a large fan had been turned on in the interior of the vehicle.

She sat up. "I'm so sorry. I didn't mean to startle you all. It was just a bad dream."

George gave her a sympathetic look. "Don't think another thing about it." He pulled a water bottle out of the cooler next to her. "Here, drink up. This should help."

She nodded and twisted off the cap before taking a couple of gulps and replacing the lid. She started to hand it back to him, but he insisted she keep it.

"You probably need to rehydrate. It's been a rough day, and you haven't eaten much. You should at least drink plenty of water, okay?"

She took the cap back off and drank several more swallows, realizing she really was pretty thirsty. She again replaced the cap and set the bottle in a nearby cup holder.

Dennis pulled back into traffic, and she looked around at the mess she'd inadvertently made.

"Sheesh. I'm so sorry about the mess. Let me help you clean it up," she said.

Jane started reaching for some papers, but George was quick to snatch them away. She didn't understand the secrecy, but she figured everyone had a right to privacy—that was, until she found a sheet with the name *George Daniels* on it, complete with his stats and a photo. It looked nothing like the man sitting before her. Before he was able to grab that one, she saw a sentence that screamed in her mind over and over.

DEATH FROM GUNSHOT WOUND.

Her eyes widened as she looked at the man pretending to be her father, her fear mounting rapidly.

He smirked at her. "Ah, well, it was a good run while it lasted."

She became angry and started to transfer that anger to her fingers, but the dangerous dark swirls wouldn't come to mind. She couldn't muster the energy to think, and suddenly, she was very, very tired.

She closed her eyes for a moment and then opened them again. "You put something in my water."

George laughed. "Didn't your mommy and daddy ever teach you not to take food from strangers?" He covered his mouth in mock surprise. "Oops! I forgot. Your mommy and daddy weren't around to teach you much of anything."

Jane did her best to glare at him, but it was taking all her effort to keep her eyes open. Before she knew it, darkness had taken over, and she was alone in her mind. She was conscious, yet she wasn't. She seemed to be trapped in the inky blackness, and she was powerless.

SEVENTEEN

Colt sat in his usual spot at The Rusty Hinge. He'd been trying to drown his sorrows in whatever alcohol James poured for him.

The gaping hole left by Jane was more than he knew how to bear. She'd chosen to leave. He wanted to understand her position. He wanted to believe she'd come back to him someday. But his heart wouldn't allow even the tiniest bit of hope to push through.

His dad had warned him about women. Colt felt the betrayal of his mom's absence almost as much as his father had.

With Jane, there was no way to even compare the two. She'd not only left him alone, but it was also as if she'd ripped his very soul from his body. He tried to concentrate on everything but Jane, yet she was all he would see when he closed his eyes.

Colt rubbed his temples. The vision of her standing before him that morning with tears falling on her beautiful cheeks made him angry with himself. He knew he had been too harsh. He should have stopped complaining and let her explain. He hadn't even gotten a kiss good-bye. He would likely never see her again. His final memories should have been of her in his arms. Maybe if he'd given her a chance, if he'd taken the time to touch her again and show her his love, she would have chosen him over her father.

He looked up at James. "Another beer."

James shook his head. "You've had more than enough, Colt. You need to go home and sleep it off. I'll call you a cab."

Colt reached across the bar and grabbed James by the shirt. "I'm not going home!"

James raised his hands in surrender. "Fine. Fine. But I'm cutting you off. I don't need you dying of alcohol poisoning in my bar."

Colt released him and sat back on his stool.

He couldn't go home. Jane wasn't there, so there was no reason to go back—ever. He continued to stare into his empty glass. He knew it wouldn't have been fair to make her choose between him and her family, but she hadn't given him any say in the matter. She was so damn stubborn.

He picked up a bottle cap from the bar and absentmindedly spun it. "I'm such an ass."

"Aw, I don't know about that, Colt. You have a cute one though."

He looked up to find a short blonde bombshell standing next to him. She was leaning on the bar, her cleavage bared for all the world to see.

She gave him a sultry smile.

He struggled to remember her name. "Nancy, right?"

She practically purred in his ear, "I knew you couldn't forget me. That one wild night last summer was more than memorable." She ran a carefully manicured finger down the length of his arm.

In the past, he would have jumped at the opportunity to spend the night with a woman like her. But no matter how hard he tried, he couldn't muster up the enthusiasm.

He didn't reply.

She pouted. "You do remember our night, don't you?"

"Yeah, I remember."

She snuggled up close, draping one arm around his shoulders. "What do you say we get out of here and go somewhere private? I'd be happy to give you an encore performance." She nipped at his ear, leaving lipstick behind.

He looked at her for a moment and then frowned. *Why was he sitting here, moping like a child, when he could be having amazing sex with this more than willing woman?*

Colt threw money on the counter and stood up. "What the hell. Let's go."

She smiled and took his hand. They walked out the door, and she pushed him, guiding him to the side of the building. Then, she backed him against the wall and kissed him. He kissed back, but it felt off. Pushing the thought away, he started to let his hands roam, but it was all wrong. Instead of getting excited, he was disgusted.

He saw Jane everywhere and in everything. This was no different.

Nancy continued to kiss him and started running her hand down to his jeans, cupping him.

He couldn't take it anymore and pushed her away. "I can't."

"What? What do you mean, you can't?"

"I just can't." His mind screamed at her, *You aren't her! I only want her!* He ran a hand through his hair. "Sorry." Then, he walked away from her.

Nancy stood behind him, stunned. When it hit her that he'd rejected her, she ran at him, her fists clenched. "How dare you, Colt Henderson! You never think of anyone but yourself!"

He stopped and turned to look at her. "No. For once, I'm thinking of someone else, and despite all that's happened, she deserves better than this from me."

Her anger grew. "Another woman? You're turning me down for someone else? There are no strings here, Colt. It's just you and me, having a lot of fun. Since when do you refuse a one-night stand?" Her eyes flashed as she yelled at him.

He gave her a sad smile. "Since I fell in love." He turned around once more and made his way to his motorcycle.

Nancy straightened her clothes and stomped back into the bar, nearly running over Peter Grant as he exited. He dodged out of her way and shook his head at her theatrics.

Seeing Colt, Peter ran toward him. "Colt! I must speak with you!"

Colt turned to see the reporter rushing toward him. His mood was surly, and his first thought was to punch Peter's lights out.

Peter stopped just short of Colt's reach and put his hands out in front of him. "Please, you need to listen. I know you're mad at me, but I've dropped the story."

Colt folded his arms in front of him. "Good. Then, we don't need to talk."

He turned to sit on his bike when Peter grabbed his arm.

"No. It's about Jane! You need to hear me out!"

Colt looked at Peter's hand on his arm.

Peter let go. "Please, give me just a moment."

"Fine, you have a minute. Go."

"I met Jane at the park this afternoon. I briefly spoke to her, but she wasn't interested in talking much, so I left. As I was leaving, I passed a blue minivan with two large men standing outside. As I entered my car, I overhead them talking. They mentioned Jane so I stopped to eavesdrop. They aren't who they say they are, Colt. They talked about chasing her for weeks and how they were glad to have finally caught her again." He took a deep breath. "One guy said he'd make her pay for all the hell she'd put him through since she ran."

Colt was struck with dread. His gut had told him that something was off, but he hadn't wanted to believe it for her sake. He'd ignored his instincts and let George take her. "Damn it! Can you describe the van in more detail?"

Peter pulled a slip of paper from his pocket and handed it to Colt. "I can do you one better. Here's the license plate. I figured it was the least I could do after the trouble I caused."

Colt scanned it and then shoved it into his pocket. He sat on his bike and fired it up. "Thanks, Peter."

"You're welcome. I hope you find her."

Colt nodded and then drove away. He needed to get home. He really shouldn't even be driving, but thankfully, his house wasn't far, and this news seemed to have sobered him up a bit. He needed lots of coffee and Dr. Weston's help.

Once Colt got home, he started the coffee pot and called his old friend. "Doc! I need you. Now."

"Whatever is the matter, boy?"

"They have Jane. That wasn't her father, and now, they have her."

Dr. Weston gasped. "I'll be right there."

Colt hung up and then called the police, explaining the situation and the conversation Peter had heard. He gave them the license plate number and demanded they do something, but he was told that if she had gone willingly, there was nothing they could do.

Minutes later, Dr. Weston burst through the door, his arms full of boxes of research. "There might be something here to help. Last night, I saw mention of The Curators. The papers made them sound more like a think tank, but after digging further, it's obvious that's a front. They own land about forty-five miles south of here."

Colt grabbed a map and spread it out on the table. Dr. Weston rifled through the papers until he found the information about the group.

Then, he studied the map. "Here!" He pushed a chubby finger on the map. "This is where it should be."

Colt drank his coffee and studied the area. It looked like all woods and back roads to him. "Are you sure, Doc? It's hard to pinpoint an address out there."

He nodded. "I'm positive. There are photos of a small building surrounded by dense forest. This is where they claimed to meet to share their research. Donald Brandt originally ran it, but he died of a sudden heart attack about ten years ago, and his successor took over. The man's name was Professor Anthony Russell. Shortly after that, the think tank was supposed to have disbanded, and the research stopped."

Colt had the horrible feeling he'd already met Professor Russell. "Do the documents describe Russell or have a photo of him?"

Dr. Weston shook his head. "No. Nothing specific about him in here. All we know is, he made administration changes and then shut the whole organization down without explanation."

Colt formulated a plan. He grabbed his hiking gear and then changed into dark clothing. While he was doing that, Dr. Weston packed food and water into a small waist pack. They loaded the gear into Dr. Weston's car.

Colt went to jump in the driver's seat, but Dr. Weston stopped him.

"Boy, you need to sleep off what's left of the alcohol in your system before you get behind the wheel." He shot Colt an accusatory look.

Dr. Weston had to bite his tongue, so he wouldn't give the young man a thorough lecture about being drunk and stupid. But Colt's father had been an old friend, and Colt was a good kid at heart. He would help Colt through this.

"You get some rest, and I'll drive. You'll need to be at your best for what lies ahead."

Jane was drifting in and out of consciousness. She strained to open her eyes, but the weight of her lids seemed to fight against it. When she did manage a peek, everything was out of focus.

As she struggled to stay awake, she saw glimpses of things that weren't there. She knew she was still in the van, but as she fought against the drug coursing through her veins, other visions took over.

She was recalling her past. She remembered being Alice Daniels.

She blinked rapidly and rubbed her eyes. The van was parked and empty, except for her. She could hear people talking just outside the window, but she wasn't able to catch most of their conversation. Snippets filtered through her haze but not enough to make sense. She lay still, listening for anything that would give her a clue as to where she was.

Then, she heard a woman's voice. It was a nasally whining sound that set her teeth on edge and provoked fear in her heart.

Julia! Oh dear God, not Julia!

Jane fought down the panic she could feel building in her chest. She took in deep breaths to control her anxiety. She remembered everything.

Julia was easily the meanest person she'd ever met. After being taken, Julia had pretended to care about her, claiming she would be her new mother. But the slightest bit of disobedience or resistance would bring out the demon hiding behind her cynical smile and large brown eyes. On a regular basis, she'd beat Jane as well as many of the other children who dared to try to stand up against her.

Then, there were the experiments. Professor Russell would put them through rounds and rounds of exhausting experiments each day, trying to find new ways to control their gifts and push them to their limits. He'd try to tell the children that they were games, but they all knew better.

During one particularly hard game, he'd pitted two of the children against each other. Little Sandra, no more than nine years old, stood in front of Jeremy. She'd trembled and cried, begging Professor Russell not to make her do this. But he had been relentless and had lacked compassion.

He'd repeated his motto, "We must do what we must do."

Jeremy had stood tall, towering over Sandra a good nine inches. He was a brave young man, and he'd kept his face passive.

Professor Russell had ordered Sandra to begin.

She'd continued to cry as she lifted her hands toward Jeremy. For just a moment, he'd dropped his stoic mask, and he'd given her a look that told her it was okay. He hadn't blamed her for what was about to happen.

She'd closed her eyes and touched him.

Jeremy did his best to endure, using his gifts to fight off the onslaught of pain Sandra transmitted through him. But her abilities had been more honed than his. She had been stronger. She was what the Professor had dubbed a *Centerpiece*, someone with remarkable abilities above and beyond the norm for their kind.

Sandra hadn't wanted to continue, but she had known that punishment would be waiting if she didn't follow through. She'd pushed back harder, and Jeremy had crumpled, writhing in pain. He had done his best not to cry out, knowing how hard it would be for Sandra if she chickened out and quit. She'd had to finish to prove her worth.

He'd clenched his teeth so hard that he actually heard one or two crack. He'd felt his body rising into the air as Sandra willed it.

Professor Russell had then ordered her to let go. She was reluctant, but when the order had been snapped at her once again, she'd flinched in fear, and she'd done as she had been told.

Jeremy had fallen a good twenty feet or so, breaking several bones in the process.

He'd spent a couple of months recovering, only to know that he'd have to endure the process again before long.

This was about the same time Jane—or rather, Alice—had realized she had to escape. She'd tried over and over to run, but they always caught her. Her punishments had included confinement to a small room during the day and starvation techniques. She had gotten a shot once a day, which she'd assumed was some sort of vitamin or nutrients to keep her alive.

As it had been drilled into them all, she had done what she must do.

She'd recovered, built her strength, and then tried to run again.

Julia had threatened to kill her several times, but she wasn't allowed that option. Alice had become a favorite. She had shown promise of unparalleled powers. She was a Centerpiece of the highest order. This had only made Julia hate her more.

The week before her final attempt to run, Julia had entered her bedroom and given her a scathing lecture on acting like a lady.

As Jane had grown, despite her surroundings, she'd blossomed. At age twenty-two, she had gotten a lot of attention—not just from the other gifted boys, but also from leading members of the society.

Julia's jealousy had run deeper than any loyalty to her organization. She'd called Jane a whore and then beaten her with a leather strap until she exhausted herself.

Her parting words had been, "There. Let's see how pretty they think you look with bruises and swelling."

Jane realized that a part of her was still Alice. That part feared these people with an intensity that she couldn't comprehend.

Each prisoner in the complex had a specialized diet, and it was strictly forbidden to share food for any reason. She'd realized that they were drugging the food according to who would and wouldn't be in the experiments that week. Those who wouldn't be participating would get higher doses to keep their abilities more subdued. Even the Centerpieces were unable to use their powers against the organization, thanks to careful planning and calculating by Professor Russell.

Jane had spent that final two weeks only eating minimal amounts to get by. She'd hidden the rest of her meals to make it appear that she'd eaten well. Then, she'd dumped it later when no one was looking. Her powers had slowly returned, bit by bit. She'd realized the shots she'd been given during her punishments were merely drugs to keep her powers on a leash.

The day she'd run, she still hadn't regained all her abilities, but by flashing a little leg and smiling at them, she'd managed to slip by the two guards keeping the main gate closed. She'd lured them into a dark corner, using the very attributes that Julia was so insanely obsessed with. Once she'd gotten them out of sight of the cameras, she'd used her gifts to render them unconscious. She had felt horrified by the thought of using her powers to hurt anyone. But as they'd stood, facing her, she'd levitated various large rocks nearby, and ironically, she'd done what she had to do.

Now, here Jane was, back in the clutches of the most evil people she'd ever known. She'd been so lost in her own head that she didn't even recognize Professor Russell when he claimed to be her father. Her stomach recoiled as she remembered him touching her in a fatherly manner and pretending to care for her. The way he'd begun to look at her in the year or two before she escaped gave her the creeps. And now that she had intimate knowledge of what that look might mean, she was determined he'd never get the chance to try to act on any of the repugnant thoughts he might be having.

With that, an image of Colt flashed in her mind. She should have listened to him. She hoped that he'd forgive her stubbornness someday. She might never see him or anyone else she cared about ever again. But one thing she knew for sure was, if she went down, she would take the whole damn bunch with her.

Her indignation for the injustices served by this group of malicious, power-hungry criminals began to build, and this time, she could feel it. As her anger compounded, she could almost feel her blood boiling. It was as if she had a fever, and her system was burning off any lasting effects of the drugs she'd ingested through the water. She concentrated on keeping that anger within, letting it work on the slivered remains of her drowsiness.

She heard Professor Russell's excited voice.

"You won't believe it. Wait until you see what she can do now. It's as if her weeks of freedom unleashed something we never knew existed. She can heal! She can stop the rain and control the breeze!"

Julia whined, "But, Andy, she's a pain in the ass. Do we really need her? We were better off without her!"

"Julia, she is integral to the future of this organization. We need her more than anyone else here. Imagine being able to control those gifts. Imagine what we could accomplish!"

Jane heard the van door open, so she held her breath and stilled her heartbeat as much as possible. She felt Professor Russell's hand grasp her calf, and she willed herself not to react.

"Alice. Alice, wake up! You're finally back home, where you belong, dearest."

She didn't move.

"Hell. Dennis! How much did you put in that bottle anyway? She's out cold!"

Dennis sounded nervous as he said, "Sorry, sir, but I wanted to be sure she would be properly contained. With the rumors and the stuff she told you she could do, I just had to know that she wouldn't be an issue."

"Well, you've succeeded. She'll have to be carried in. See to it."

Jane heard Professor Russell and Julia talking as they walked away while Dennis carefully reached in the back. He put his arms around her and pulled her limp body from the seat. She continued her pretense of being unconscious, while she planned her next move.

EIGHTEEN

MY RAGE IS LOOSED,

AND THOSE WHO'VE WRONGED US WILL BE PUT IN THEIR PLACE.

Colt and Dr. Weston had driven as far as the dirt road would allow while still keeping them out of sight from the deceptively small compound laid out before them. Colt had a knife encased in his boot, and he'd tucked a 9mm Glock in the waistband of his jeans. He didn't know what kind of trouble he'd run into, but he was as prepared as he would ever be.

Dr. Weston placed a hand on Colt's shoulder. "Be careful. These people might be capable of anything."

Colt, in a moment of impulse, pulled the older man into a quick hug. "Take care, Doc. Remember, if I'm not back within an hour, get the hell out of here."

Dr. Weston nodded. "I will."

Colt carefully made his way to the tall fence surrounding the property and watched as two men walked the fence line. He climbed a tree and precariously perched himself on a thick limb close to the gate. Once the guards were out of sight, he launched himself over the gate, narrowly missing the iron protruding from the top. He landed with a thud and quickly got up and moving before someone could come to check out any possible noises they might have heard.

He cautiously approached the building, staying hidden as much as possible. He admitted that, on the outside, it looked much like a small office building with a bay door for something as seemingly innocuous as paper or supply deliveries. But he suspected the reality was much more problematic. He saw the bay door open, so he ducked down behind a pile of large rocks and watched.

A van matching the description Peter had given him pulled up next to the door. Colt had to restrain his need to run in, his gun blazing, and get her out. But at this point, he didn't even know if she was still in there.

The sun was quickly setting, and it was going to be a challenge to keep everything and everyone in view.

A tall woman emerged from the now open door and put her hands on her hips. Her body language indicated she was impatient and maybe annoyed. When the van doors opened, he saw two men he didn't recognize and the man who pretended to be Jane's father. Jane didn't climb out behind them, and Colt once again had to fight the urge to rush in and find her.

Colt was far enough away that he couldn't clearly hear the conversation between the woman and the fake Mr. Daniels, but he knew women well enough to tell she was not happy.

She pointed at the van. He gestured to it as well. Then, she crossed her arms and appeared to pout. Fake Mr. Daniels turned around and reached into the van. Whatever he was doing, it wasn't working out like he'd planned, so he yelled at someone named Dennis. The larger man came forward, spoke for a moment, and then reached into the van himself.

Colt gripped the rock in front of him as he saw Dennis pull back with an unconscious Jane in his arms.

Slipping closer to them, he flattened his back against the wall and pulled out his gun. He didn't know how many more were inside, but he had enough rounds to kill every damn one of them standing there, if necessary.

He heard the woman gasp in outrage.

"What has happened to her? She's…she's—"

Professor Russell smiled. "She's blossomed, Julia."

Julia growled her displeasure. "She's not a flower, Andy. She's a weapon. It would serve you well to remember that."

Dennis looked concerned. "Uh, Professor? I don't think she's breathing."

Professor Russell pushed past Julia and grabbed Jane's wrist. He couldn't find a pulse. "You moron! You gave her too much! You might have killed her!"

Julia cackled and gave the limp girl a disgusted look. "Thank God."

Professor Russell turned to Julia. "You idiot! Why can't you understand that we need her?" He turned to Dennis. "Lay her down. I'll need to administer CPR."

Dennis gingerly placed her body on the dirt-packed drive and stepped back.

Colt prepared to spring into action.

As Professor Russell leaned over her, her eyes shot open. He recoiled, quickly noting that her irises were almost the color of her hair.

She pushed her arms out in front of her, throwing the three people standing before her back against the building. She stood, staring at them.

Her hair ruffled as the wind began to whip into a frenzy, picking up dirt as it gathered around her.

Colt could hear shouts coming from inside the building, but the dust had kicked up so bad that he could barely see anything past Jane. He took that moment to bolt toward her, calling her name.

Jane turned her head toward him, and with one hand, she held him in place. Quickly realizing it was Colt, she released her grasp and the intensity in her eyes softened.

Colt reached her side, gun in hand, and smiled at her.

She raised her hands once more, and dust became a solid wall, floating in place. She grabbed Colt's hand and slowly started backing away from the building. She knew that wouldn't hold Professor Russell and his men off for long. They'd worked far too hard to find her, and they wouldn't let her slip away again without a fight.

As if on cue, shots rang out, and bullets pierced through the barrier she'd erected in front of them. She could hear yelling on the other side and assumed Professor Russell was again trying to convince his cohorts she was valuable to them only if she was alive. More shots were fired, and she pulled Colt to her, tightly wrapping her arms around him.

When she was sure the rain of bullets was over, she again grabbed his hand, and they bolted for the gate.

Colt frantically ran through the various ways to get it open, knowing that it would be mere moments before Professor Russell and his men caught up, wall or no wall.

Jane already had it covered. As they neared the gate, she pushed her right hand forward and flicked her middle and ring finger inward. In that instant, the large iron gate flew off its hinges as if it were as light as a feather.

Colt smiled as they both took off into a full sprint. *God, I love her!*

They reached Dr. Weston's car, and he already had the engine running. They jumped in the backseat, and he pulled away as quickly as he could, leaving a cloud of dust behind him. They drove for several minutes before they heard gunshots.

Jane turned to Dr. Weston and instructed him to keep driving. Then, she turned in her seat and peered out the back window. Just as she was about to once again display her abilities, a bullet hit a rear tire, and Dr. Weston lost control of the car. He struggled to keep the vehicle on the road, but it ended up pitching into a steep ditch before coming to an abrupt stop.

Colt checked on Jane, and upon seeing she was fine, he moved to Dr. Weston next. He was okay but badly shaken.

Jane kicked out the side window and started to climb out. "You guys stay put. I've got this."

Colt shook his head. "Not happening, beautiful. I'm coming with you."

She glared at him but then continued to make her way out of the car and onto the road with Colt directly behind her. She stood in the middle of the dirt pathway, looking at the oncoming van.

It stopped short of reaching them, and Professor Russell stepped out with his hands in the air.

She looked at Colt once more. "Please, get back to the car. Protect Dr. Weston."

Her expression and the determination in her eyes told him all he needed to know.

Colt moved closer and pulled her to him for a quick kiss. Then, he nodded and started walking backward. "You got this, sweetheart. Give 'em hell."

He ran back to the car and helped Dr. Weston maneuver out of the tilted vehicle. Then, they both watched as Jane continued to stare down Professor Russell.

"Turn around and leave, Professor Russell! It's the only way you'll walk away alive." Her voice was menacing.

"Ah, dearest. Let's discuss this like rational adults, shall we?"

"Sure. Should I drug you first, as you did me? Or would you prefer I lock you in a room and starve you for days? Maybe we could play one of your many games."

Professor Russell looked nervous.

"I think I rather like that idea. Let's play one of your games. We could reenact the game you forced Jeremy and Sandra to play—over and over and over." Her sneer showed her teeth.

He could visibly see her fury mounting by the look on her face. "Please, think about this. We are trying to help people. Our purpose is to build an invincible army that could put an end to all wars. We could stop hunger and famine! We could rule the earth in peace! We could help the human race become more civilized."

She released a harsh laugh. "No, it's not about furthering the human race. You have no interest in that. You'd prefer to enslave them instead."

At that moment, she heard the whiz of a tranquilizer gun somewhere from her left.

Jane turned toward the sound, and with a look, she stopped the dart in its tracks. It fell to the ground, landing just beside her. She stepped sideways, crushing it under her foot.

She glanced up and smiled. "Nice try, Professor Russell. It's a shame it didn't work." She glanced at Dennis, noticing the weapon and tranquilizers in his hand. "It's so very like you to have someone else do your dirty work."

Dennis dropped his weapon and stepped back into the trees, fearing for his life. Once he was out of sight, she heard him running away.

Professor Russell cleared his throat. "My, how you've changed in such a short time, dearest."

"Don't ever call me dearest again."

"So sorry. My mistake." He took a couple of steps forward.

"Don't move, Professor Russell! I'm not kidding!"

Professor Russell smiled. "It's just you and me now. Why can't we work this out?"

Her eyes flashed. "I'll never work with the likes of you ever again."

He shook his head. "No, you've got it all wrong. The only way to change this situation is for you to kill me. That's not who you are. You simply don't have it in you, Alice."

She smiled at him, and her hatred for him and all he stood for practically radiated off of her.

"Too bad for you I'm not Alice anymore."

She spread her hands out to her sides, palms forward, and lifted her face to the sky. The sun seemed to maneuver itself simply to shine on her alone. The wind began to pick up, and dark clouds started rolling in behind her. Lightning cracked across the sky, bringing with it an intense rumbling that shook the earth.

She looked at him and whispered, "I am Jane."

Though it was a whisper, her voice carried on the wind and reached Professor Russell as if it were a shout. He started backing up, true fear evident on his face for the first time.

She pulled her arms inward, and the trees seemed to reach for Professor Russell, trying to grab him. He ran then, his panic causing him to stumble.

She walked toward the van, and as she pushed forward, the sky above her rotated and twisted.

Dr. Weston and Colt observed from their place near the car, experiencing the event, but they were not in any obvious danger. She had it contained to focus solely on her target.

Colt watched in astonishment.

Dr. Weston's mouth was hanging open. He looked at Colt with eyes so wide that they appeared to barely stay in their sockets. "What the hell?"

Colt held in an inappropriate laugh as he witnessed the always proper doctor losing his decorum. He turned his face to the wind and smiled. "You said it, Doc. She's damn amazing."

Jane inclined her head forward, and the funnel cloud above her moved to the van, tossing it out of her way. It continued moving forward, clearing a path for her.

Professor Russell attempted to run, but as he heard the thunderous noise behind him, he turned. His vision was filled with the image of an angry young woman with fire-red hair surrounding her like a halo. The storm around her was at her command, and she was sending it after him. The funnel spat out the van and then continued in his direction like a heat-seeking missile.

As the darkness surrounded him, Professor Russell looked at Jane one last time. He gazed at the face that once was full of love and compassion for all, and he realized that she would now be his undoing.

NINETEEN

NO LONGER DO I RUN FROM SHADOWS. WHEN THEY CALL HER NAME,

I SCREAM BACK, "I AM JANE!"

Jane stood in the middle of the road, watching the wind and rain sweeping away all that had corrupted her existence.

She hadn't seen what happened to Professor Russell, but she didn't believe there was any way he could have survived the cascade of fury she'd just thrown his way. It had been building for years, and today, she'd found the strength to take a stand and face her fears. She fully expected that, in a few days, the news would be full of stories about the freak storm that had carried his body miles away.

Her heart was pounding so loudly that it seemed to drown out any other noises surrounding her. She briefly thought about those still left at the compound. She wondered if Sandra and Jeremy were still there. Her heart ached as she ran down a list of names and faces she'd left behind so many weeks ago.

Jane turned to see Colt and Dr. Weston approaching.

Colt smiled at her, but it was quickly replaced by a frown. "Jane? Are you okay?"

She nodded slowly, but she felt herself fading into blackness. Colt wrapped his arms around her and noted the blood running from her ears. She was also starting to bleed from her nose.

"Doc! We need to get her to the hospital now!"

Dr. Weston moved toward his car but instantly turned back. "Colt, we don't have a vehicle anymore."

Colt let out a string of obscenities, and then he picked her up and carried her to the side of the road. He sat down in a soft patch of grass, holding her in his lap. "Jane, sweetheart, open your eyes. Look at me."

She blinked slowly and then smiled up at him. "Colt."

"I'm here, beautiful."

She reached up and touched his face. "I thought you hated me."

He shook his head. "Never. I could never hate you. I was just angry. I didn't mean anything I said, Jane."

She closed her eyes. "It's okay."

He pulled her closer. "No, it's not okay. Do you hear me? It's not okay. I need you, damn it. I need you. I love you, Jane."

Her smile was weak, but she did her best to let the love she felt for him push through her fingers as they continued to touch his face. He felt the sensation on his cheeks, and then it flowed through his body as she smiled at him. Once more, she had rendered him speechless.

A single tear escaped, and gravity pulled it toward her ear. "I'll always love you, Colt. Nothing could ever change that." She closed her eyes again.

He leaned down to kiss her. His lips touched hers, but she didn't respond.

He pulled back and examined her face. "Jane?"

He gave her a gentle shake. "Jane! Jane!"

She wasn't responding.

Dr. Weston rushed over. "I've called nine-one-one. An ambulance will be here as soon as possible."

Colt looked up, tears running down his face. "I don't think she's breathing, Doc!"

Dr. Weston frowned and reached to touch her neck, looking for a pulse. When he couldn't find one there, he tried her wrist. His face dropped.

"No! She's not dead! She can't be! Save her, Doc! Save her now!" Colt was near hysterics.

"Colt, I don't think there's anything I can do. You forget, she's not like us."

Colt pulled her to him, rocking her in his arms. "No!" His tears turned to sobs. "Please, God, no! Not her! Take me, but leave her!"

Dr. Weston touched Colt's shoulder, but he was inconsolable. In the distance, sirens could be heard, growing to a deafening level as the ambulance approached.

An EMT jumped out and surveyed the destruction around them. "What happened here?"

Dr. Weston snapped his fingers at the young man. "This woman needs medical attention immediately!"

Dr. Weston looked at Colt cradling Jane in his arms and jumped into action. He had to convince Colt to let the EMTs take her. "They have the equipment and supplies she needs. I don't have any of those things with me, and to be honest, I fear I'm not steady enough to think straight. I'm too close to her Colt. They need to put her in the ambulance so they can help her."

Colt reluctantly let them load her into the ambulance, and he watched as they took her vitals. The grim look on their faces sent Colt into another fit of rage.

Dr. Weston had to step in between Colt and the ambulance, placing a hand on his chest. "Let them do their job, Colt. If she can be helped, her best chance is with them."

Colt screamed at Jane then, "You can't leave me again! You promised, it'd be okay!"

The EMTs looked at him in alarm and then at each other before slamming the doors. They raced away with Jane's lifeless body, and Colt fell to his knees in the middle of the dirt road. He stared at the vehicle until it turned onto the highway, disappearing from his sight.

A few days later, Dr. Weston was making his rounds when he spotted Colt asleep in a chair in the waiting room. He walked over and sat down. "Colt, wake up, son."

"Huh? What? I'm up." Colt scrubbed his face with his hands, trying to force his expression to cooperate with his poorly told lie.

Dr. Weston frowned. "You really look like crap, boy. You should be sleeping at home."

"No, I'm good. I just dozed off."

A sigh escaped Dr. Weston's lips. "You won't change anything by being here all the time."

"I know. But when she wakes up, I want to be the first thing she sees."

Dr. Weston shook his head. "*If* she wakes up, Colt. We simply don't know at this point."

Colt shook his head in denial. "No. She'll wake up. She just needs time to heal." His eyes rose to meet Dr. Weston's. "I have to believe it, Doc. I refuse to believe anything else."

The older man nodded. "Okay." He looked down at the chart in his hands. "I wanted to let you know that they're done with the scan, so you can go back in if you like."

Colt nodded and rose from his chair. He patted Dr. Weston on the back as he passed.

His thoughts reeled as he made his way down the familiar corridor. When he reached Jane's room, he fought the urge to knock. His mind rushed back to the first time he'd visited her here and how she'd answered his knock with the most mesmerizing voice he'd ever heard.

He pushed through the door and gazed at her comatose form. Intrusive wires, tubes, and machines surrounded her. He wanted to shake her and force her to wake up, but he knew that would do no good. Jane only did things on her timeline.

He leaned over her and tenderly kissed her forehead. Then, he settled down in the chair next to her bed and picked up a book. He'd been reading out loud to her every day. It was an erotic spoof he'd found at the local thrift store.

He smiled at her. "You really need to wake up, beautiful. We're just getting to the good part, and you don't want to miss it."

Jane didn't stir or respond.

Colt listened to the beeping of the monitor in the background for a moment. Then, he opened the book to the bookmarked page and began to read.

Later that evening, Colt was awakened by an odd whirring sound coming from the hallway. He sat up and stretched, taking a moment to realize where he was. The lights were dim, and the chair he'd been in for most of the day was becoming increasingly uncomfortable.

He stood and stretched again, recognizing the familiar sound of the janitor waxing the floor. He gazed down at Jane. She still looked the same.

Colt brushed a stray hair from her face. "I'm starting to lose hope, sweetheart. I need a sign, something to show me that you're still with me." He took her hand in his. "I'll wait forever if that's what it takes, but I just need to know you haven't moved on without me."

He kissed the back of her hand and then gently placed it on her stomach.

Entering the bathroom, he turned on the faucet and washed his face. As he stared at his haggard appearance in the mirror, he tried to give himself a pep talk. "You gotta hang in there for her. Don't give up yet."

He turned off the light and stepped back into the room. When he turned, something soft flew by his head and hit the door. Frowning, he bent down and picked up the small teddy bear he'd purchased in the gift shop a few days ago.

He turned again to see yet another small stuffed animal being hurled at his head. He caught this one—a white rabbit that had been sent by Dr. Weston.

"You know, if you're gonna read me dirty books, at least have the decency to pick one that isn't a parody. *The Humping Games*? Really, Colt?"

He rushed to her bedside and smiled as she looked up at him. Her eyes were bright and vivid. He nearly launched himself at her as he hugged her. When he lifted his head, the relief was obvious on his face.

Colt pointed to the book. "That's quality entertainment! I'm enjoying it!" His smile faded. "You scared the hell out of me."

Jane's voice softened as she said, "I'm sorry, Colt. I guess I just needed time to heal."

He smiled broadly once again. "That's what I told, Doc, but he was less sure. He doesn't know you like I do."

She grinned and motioned for him to come closer. He leaned down, and she placed a gentle kiss on his lips. When he pulled back, she saw a trace of tears.

He cradled her face in his hands. "I didn't know how I was going to go on without you."

She touched his hand and closed her eyes. "Thankfully, you don't have to."

He kissed her again, but they were interrupted by a nurse.

She gasped at the sight of Jane sitting up in bed. "Oh, dear!" She excitedly ran out the door, calling for Dr. Weston.

Colt and Jane laughed as they heard her shouts echoing down the halls.

Jane looked up at him again. "Did you bring any cards with you?"

He looked confused. "Cards? No. Why?"

"I do believe, the last time we were here, you promised to teach me strip poker."

He wiggled his eyebrows at her. "You get better, and I'll not only teach you, but I'll also let you win."

She laughed again and reached for his hands. Her face turned serious. "Colt? What about the others? Did anyone save them?"

He frowned. "The police went back to the compound, but it was empty. It appears that hateful woman, and whoever is left to follow her, skipped town and took your friends with them."

Her disappointment was obvious. "I have to find them, Colt. I have to help them." She looked at their entwined fingers. "I remember it all, and I can't allow that organization to continue to hurt innocent people"

"Don't worry, Jane. We'll find them." He gave her hand a reassuring squeeze.

Jane prayed Colt was right.

COMING SOON!

SHADOWS OF DECEPTION

(THE SHADOWS TRILOGY, BOOK TWO)

MARCH 2016

The Shadows

by Amy Hale

I run from shadows.

They call my name and taunt me with their cries.

I search for truth, within and without,

Yet I see nothing but lies.

New faces surround and invite me in,

But is my trust in vain?

Confusion follows me wherever I go,

And I often feel insane.

Why is life so complicated?

And where does one begin?

When all I know is upside down,

I fear I'll never win.

Angels and demons on either side,

I know not where to turn.

But then I hurt the ones I love,

My shame and anger burn.

amy hale

FORGIVENESS FLOWS FREE, AND FEAR ABATES.

I CLING TO HIS DEAR SOUL.

FOR NOW, I RUN SO FAR AWAY,

AND PRAY I FIND CONTROL.

MY STEPS ARE HEAVY, AS IS MY HEART,

THE PAIN, IT CALLS FOR DEATH.

YET I FIND FRIENDS TO HELP ME UP.

THEY HELP ME CATCH MY BREATH.

ONCE MORE, I TRY TO SHINE THE LIGHT,

TO MAKE THE SHADOWS FLEE.

BUT SHADOWS COME IN MANY FORMS,

THEY CLAIM TO COMFORT ME.

NOW APPROACHES THE MOMENT I'VE WAITED FOR.

MY STRUGGLES ARE NEARING AN END.

YET TO TRUST THE ONE AND LEAVE THE OTHER,

I'LL LOSE MORE THAN A FRIEND.

DECEIT MADE PLAIN AND FOES EXPOSED,

I STRUGGLE WITH HER FACE.

MY RAGE IS LOOSED,

AND THOSE WHO'VE WRONGED US WILL BE PUT IN THEIR PLACE.

NO LONGER DO I RUN FROM SHADOWS. WHEN THEY CALL HER NAME,

I SCREAM BACK, "I AM JANE!"

ACKNOWLEDGMENTS

I am eternally grateful to all those who have encouraged me during the process of this book. I could never have finished this without the support and help of so many people.

As always, my husband and children are my rock. John, you continued to push me to believe in myself, even when I struggled with so much doubt. You will never know how much that means to me. Matt and Rachel, thanks for your understanding and patience when I felt like I was losing my mind and for all the cool music recommendations. Rachel, thanks for helping me figure out my playlist as I worked through this manuscript.

Again, I thank my parents and siblings for promoting and cheering me on. You all are the best and I love you dearly! My mother was a huge inspiration while writing this story and I regret that she never got to see it finished, but I know she was proud of me and what I'm trying to accomplish. I've never seen anyone face cancer with the courage and composure displayed by my dear mamma. I hope to be like her when I grow up.

Many thanks to my beta readers—Lana, Jan, Tania, Paula, Ailsa, Kari, Jess, Becky, Anne, and Amber. You gals really helped me keep it together! A big thanks also goes out to Ailsa and Trish for helping me proofread. I couldn't have done this without any of you amazing ladies!

Special thanks to Anne Hartory for her expertise as I worked through Jane's medical issues and healing. Jane isn't your average patient so I had to twist reality a bit, but Anne kept me as close as possible! I couldn't have done this without you sweet lady!

I certainly can't forget Jovana Shirley and her fantastic editing and gorgeous formatting! Thanks for making me look good!

Sarah Hanson, thanks for the amazing cover! Your talent and vision inspire me!

I owe a special thanks to my Red Coat PR family and my author friends, A.L. Woods and Sarah J. Pepper. I can't begin to express my gratitude for your help and encouragement!

Last but not least, thank you, dear readers. Without you, I'd be lost. Because of you, I've been able to breathe life into a dream that I feared would never come true. I might write the stories, but you are the wonderful people who really make the magic happen. My eternal thanks for your continued support!

ABOUT THE AUTHOR

Amy Hale is an Oklahoma native now living in Illinois. Her husband and two children are the center of her universe even though her cat believes otherwise. She's been writing stories and poems since childhood, providing an outlet for her active imagination. She loves music, reading, writing, and photography. Amy believes that happiness comes from surrounding yourself with people you love, helping others, and being content with your current place in the world.

BE SURE TO SIGN UP FOR AMY'S NEWSLETTER ON HER WEBSITE, SO YOU DON'T MISS THE LATEST UPDATES AND ANNOUNCEMENTS.

YOU CAN FIND AMY IN THE FOLLOWING PLACES:

WEBSITE: WWW.AUTHORAMYHALE.COM

FACEBOOK: WWW.FACEBOOK.COM/AUTHORAMYHALE

TWITTER: @AUTHORAMYHALE

NOVEL SAMPLE OF SNOW WHITE LIES BY SARAH J. PEPPER

FOR MORE INFORMATION ABOUT SARAH'S AMAZING WORK, CHECK OUT HER WEBSITE: WWW.SARAHJPEPPER.COM

"Evil poisons everyone. Period. Our mouths water when we sink our teeth into what we have always craved. Surrendering to our desires by biting off a delectable piece of the forbidden fruit is nothing more than a meager confession: Poison tastes sinfully sweet,"— Confessions of the Big Apple Debutante, by blogger Miss Snow White.

PROLOGUE

{New York City, Imminent Future in the 21st Century}
{*Alias: Snow White*}

The provocative scent of the once unnamed vigilante lingered on my chiffon curtains. Motorcycle exhaust mixed with his signature cologne. Other than his aphrodisiac essence, there was no other indication that he'd been inside my penthouse tonight. Even so, I knew he'd been here all night to protect me from the *Seven*, a demonic mob that claimed New York City for their Queen.

Drawing back the curtains, I gazed through the balcony windows that overlooked the Big Apple. The city was particularly enchanting when the sun cast vibrant hues over the brilliant architecture built by our forefathers—unremarkable commoners who'd been long forgotten by all but one. The *Huntsman* bore witness to the rise and fall of nations, oversaw queens and kings come to power, and had washed more blood off his hands than any wartime criminal. Yet, he was never mentioned in textbooks, on the news, or God forbid, the tabloids. He might as well have been a ghost for he'd claimed no name for nearly two centuries. The Huntsman was the most unrenowned person alive; yet, he pestered my every waking thought.

The natural beauty of the skyline *almost* overshadowed the fact that the city was diseased with black magic: alchemy of Seventh degree. Nevertheless, a debutante such as myself, could pretend the necromantic sickness enslaving the city did not exist. The fashion, propaganda, high-end lifestyle, limelight, and little *white lies* were enough to ignore the evil festering in the city below. Furthermore, half of the city paid dues to White Industries. *My* Enterprise. My credit cards had no balance limit because of the good fortune this city had provided me.

However, I knew that the Huntsman saw a different scene gazing upon the greatest city on Earth. It was a city that came with power; a city that thrived off of the almighty dollar; a city that brewed with dark magic. It was the city to which he had been condemned to so long ago by the Queen who swore no allegiance to the Americans.

If I closed my eyes, I could picture him leaning against the bronzed casing of the window beside me. I envisioned him looking down at the citizens with a vengeful jealousy. They lived the lives they wanted. He did not.

Yet, he had come for me on his own accord.

That he was in my penthouse tonight was not to be mistaken with his newfound freedom. No, it wasn't a simple coincidence that what he was ordered to do and what he so desperately sought were one and the same.

Me.

I let out a gasp upon catching sight of him. Blanketed by shadows, he watched me from outside on the balcony. His frozen breath lingered in with the industries' smoke that capped the sky. By all means, he could hide in plain sight, even though his robust stature suggested otherwise. I eyed his leather jacket and wished that I clung to his body instead of it.

Hunger had long since manifested in his light blue eyes when he gazed at me. I'd promised to slip into something more comfortable the next time we met, but nothing in my closet justified tonight's significance. Hence, cherry lipstick and pair of black *Burberry* heels had to do.

The mix of lust and the forbidden four-letter word built between us until I could no longer stand it. I stepped out from behind the softness of the curtains and pushed open the oversized door. The harshness of the bitter cold air pricked my skin, but the temperature was miniscule to the effect he had on me.

My choice of attire, or lack thereof, was met with unhinged approval in his eyes. His gaze dropped. His body tensed. He was at war with himself; he was in battle with me. My arsenal was in the form of lipstick, and his were clenched tightly in his hands. One gripped a black powder gun, circa the Revolutionary War. The other clutched a bright red apple. Fate brought us together, but it would be his choice to comply with the evilness that forced us against each other.

My stiletto switchblades clicked against the icy floor as I approached him. For a city that never slept, everything else was drowned out when I met him on the edge. Without tearing his gaze from my lips, he handed me the apple. His cold hand lingered on mine until I punctured the fruit's skin with my manicured nails. The juices dripped down my arm as I brought it to my mouth.

"Just one bite," the Huntsman promised. His archaic Americana accent expelled the urgency in his voice with a lingering provocativeness that could not be matched.

I knew I shouldn't do as he asked. The apple was laced with poison that would certainly be my undoing. Yet, to deny my cravings any longer would positively kill me.

The sweet apple burst in my mouth. As I swallowed the forbidden fruit, he closed the gap between us, taking what he desired. With the gun pressed up against my body, he stole a kiss from me—a kiss I had no intention of denying him.

With the gun's nozzle resting against me, I dropped the lipstick-stained apple. It fell off the edge of the balcony just as a gunshot broke the stillness of the night.

Made in the USA
Charleston, SC
03 September 2016